Mike is sixteen and a guy.

Mike thinks about sex
roughly every other second,
which he's pretty sure is normal.
So now he's just . . . got more options.
It's not that bad, right?

Theoretically, it should be
awesome.

what

a novel by

ever.

s. j. goslee

SQUARE
FISH

Roaring Brook Press
New York

for my boys,
sullivan and flynn

**SQUARE
FISH**

An imprint of Macmillan Publishing Group, LLC
175 Fifth Avenue
New York, NY 10010
fiercereads.com

Square Fish and the Square Fish logo are trademarks of Macmillan and
are used by Roaring Brook Press under license from Macmillan.

Our books may be purchased in bulk for promotional, educational, or
business use. Please contact your local bookseller or the Macmillan
Corporate and Premium Sales Department at (800) 221-7945 ext. 5442
or by e-mail at MacmillanSpecialMarkets@macmillan.com.

Library of Congress Cataloging-in-Publication Data

Names: Goslee, S. J., author.
Title: Whatever : a novel / by S.J. Goslee.
Description: New York : Roaring Brook Press, 2016. | Summary: Junior
   year is going to be the best ever for slacker Mike until he loses his
   girlfriend, gets roped into school activities, and becomes totally confused
   about his sexual orientation after sharing a drunken kiss with a guy.
Identifiers: LCCN 2015023376 | ISBN 978-1-250-11514-0 (paperback)
   ISBN 978-1-62672-400-6 (ebook)
Subjects: | CYAC: Friendship—Fiction. | Coming out (Sexual orientation)—
   Fiction. | Gays—Fiction. | Dating (Social customs)—Fiction. | High
   schools—Fiction. | Schools—Fiction. | Humorous stories. | BISAC:
   JUVENILE FICTION / Love & Romance. | JUVENILE NONFICTION /
   Boys & Men. | JUVENILE FICTION / Humorous Stories.
Classification: LCC PZ7.1.G674 Wh 2016 | DDC [Fic]—dc23
LC record available at http://lccn.loc.gov/2015023376

Originally published in the United States by Roaring Brook Press
First Square Fish edition: 2017
Book designed by Andrew Arnold
Square Fish logo designed by Filomena Tuosto

1   3   5   7   9   10   8   6   4   2

LEXILE: 910L

one.

Mike Tate is currently more than a little obliterated. Something to do with the cheap beer and excellent pot. He's lounging poolside in between his girlfriend, Lisa, and his buddy, Jason, with the fire pit at his back. The August air is hazy and thick with heat, and Mike blinks blearily up at the tiki torches framing the sliding glass doors.

Cam Scott's house is bigger than it looks from the front. It's a split level, with a sprawling den and a finished basement that opens up onto a yard that's a good three-fourths of an acre, butting up against miles of Morrison Township woods. Add that to the fact that Cam's dad doesn't care how rowdy they get, so long as the police don't get involved, and it's the perfect place to party.

It's the last party of the summer—arguably the *best* party of the summer. Cam has spared no expense; there are twinkle lights and monster packs of Twizzlers, and Cam's older brother, Zack, is still grilling up burgers, even though it's going on three in the morning.

There's music blaring out of the sound system hooked up

underneath the deck. It's power pop, but Mike's in the mood to take it. His junior year looms on the horizon, just a few days away, and he's betting on it being pretty fucking sweet.

There are three things about his life that Mike wouldn't change—ever, for anything.

One: his little sister, Rosie. She drives him up a wall sometimes, but she's a trip, and she's started dressing like him, working holes into her jeans and scribbling black magic marker all over her tees. Mike totally approves.

Two: his crappy garage band. He loves those dudes. They're kind of the best, especially Cam. He's a dick, but he's as close to a brother as Mike's going to get.

Three: uh, three—something to do with Lisa. Lisa is the *coolest*.

He says all this to Lisa, flashing her a grin. "Everything else can just bite me."

two.

August ends abruptly, like someone sucker punched it in the face and it went down sobbing like a little girl, segueing into a soggy, muggy September. Mike manages to survive his first week of eleventh grade at South Morrison High—barely, and mostly because of the awesomeness of Zack Scott and his homegrown weed. Zack's got a walk-in closet in his attic bedroom that acts as a makeshift greenhouse, also home to his three-foot iguana, Alfie.

After school lets out on Friday, Mike's mom heads off with Rosie—dinner and a trip to Build-a-Bear as a reward for not making any of the other kids cry during her first week of first grade—and he takes full advantage of the empty house with Meckles and Cam and a baggie of Zack's finest.

Mike likes to think he's popular. He's in a sort-of-band with three other popular dudes and Jason, who is barely cool by association, but they let him hang because he's the only one who knows how to even turn on the Casio. With all those switches and buttons, Mike always ends up getting it stuck on Extreme Gothic Organ or something.

Popularity's subjective, of course, but Mike maintains that he's pretty fucking awesome. "I am so fucking awesome," Mike says, lying upside down on his bed, head hanging off the edge. His arms are dangling, hands brushing the carpet. It feels rough—a slight, hot burn when he drags his knuckles along the pile. "Unlike you losers."

Cam's wearing a truly spectacular Hawaiian shirt with a purple-pink sunset and silhouettes of palm trees—it's one of the better ones in his collection, and admittedly works well with his shaggy haircut, which Cam calls his "sweet locks." He shoves Mike's shoulder with his foot. "Fuck you."

Mike says, "You wish," halfheartedly smacking at Cam's toes. Mike and Cam have been stuck with each other since kindergarten. In certain circles they're labeled as best friends, and they're even occasionally mistaken for actual brothers—both of them are on the brownish side of blond and on the short side of tall, but Cam is stocky and broad-shouldered, thicker where all Mike's parts are lean.

Cam shoves harder at Mike's side and Mike slips off the mattress and lands on his neck and elbows, knees against his chest, spine curving, stretched muscles just shy of painful. This is some weird flexibility he's got going on here. Mike's sure it should probably hurt more than it does.

He huffs and twists and falls onto his side, cheek mashed into the carpet. It smells funny. Maybe they should let up smoking weed in his room. Or maybe he should vacuum more than once a year.

He fishes his phone out of his pocket and thumbs on the display. 6:50 p.m. He's somehow lost four hours. His mouth tastes like dead things, his tongue feels like cotton, and he thinks that somewhere in there he had a conversation with Omar about Jason's fingers and Cheez-Its and those giant spiders from Harry Potter. *Shit*. He must have called Omar.

Meckles, a killer drummer and Mike's other best bro, is sprawled lazily in Mike's desk chair, his large body barely fitting between the armrests. Mike groans and tugs on Meckles' outstretched leg, fingers snagging his ankle. "You let me call Omar," he says. They're such *assholes*. Omar probably thinks he's the biggest dumbass; why does he always end up calling him when he's stoned?

Meckles snickers.

Mike rolls to his feet and sniffs his armpits. He's kind of rank, and he contemplates taking a half-assed shower before switching out his T-shirt for something that isn't three days old.

Fuck it. He's already late to meet Lisa.

"See you dudes later," he says, and Cam gives him a two-finger salute.

"I'm not actually your girlfriend," Lisa says, leaning across their table at the diner to flick Mike's ear right in the middle of his rant about how Cam and Meckles are such douche bags for letting him call Omar at *work*. "I don't have to put up with this."

Lisa would technically be Mike's best friend if Mike was the kind of guy who had girls for best friends. That sort of thing had stopped being cool back in sixth grade, and when it circled around into being cool again, Mike had already alienated Lisa with years of ignorance and sticking gum in her hair. Which, of course, all culminated with them making out at Cam's last New Year's party. There had been the excited buzz of the countdown and they'd been squished up next to each other on the couch at the time; that's Mike's only explanation.

"We're dating, though," Mike says as he dips a fry into his chocolate shake.

Lisa rolls her eyes. "I let you buy me dinner and sometimes we make out a little when we're bored. That's not dating."

"Okay." Mike bobs his head, rolling with it. "Then you can pay for the movie."

"Deal," she says, and then takes a huge bite out of her hamburger.

Mike pauses with a fry at his lips. "Wait, seriously?" They're *really* not dating?

Lisa chews and chews and chews for as long as possible, head tilted, a pensive look on her face. Then she says, "I kind of want to ask Larson out."

"Larson Kemp?" Mike says, incredulous. "The creepy dude who wears suspenders and hangs out with Casper

Jorgenson behind the gym, making craploads of origami frogs?"

Lisa smiles. "He's so handsome."

Mike kicks her shin under the table. "You're full of shit."

"I'm serious, Michael," Lisa says, still grinning. "All you do is smoke up and forget to shower. I'm better off with someone I'm less likely to get a communicable disease from."

Mike narrows his eyes at her. After the surprise kiss on New Year's Eve, Lisa had made Mike apologize for shoving a salamander down her dress when they'd been eleven. She'd made him apologize in front of Meckles and *Cam*. It's been eight months since then, since they reconciled their differences and started fooling around. Mike wishes he'd known that he and Lisa were apparently just friends with benefits—though, since they've never actually had anything remotely close to sex, Lisa would probably destroy him for just the implication. But now he feels like he's wasted all this time. "Well," Mike says, slumping lower in the booth. "This sucks."

"It doesn't. I just need you to stop complaining about Omar's work schedule and Cam's porn and Jason's track practice," she says. "It's getting old. Maybe you need new friends."

"Maybe you need a new face," Mike says, scowling, crossing his arms over his chest.

"I'm not kidding about Larson," Lisa says. "I bet he'd take me to cool German restaurants. Did you know his dad owns a boat?"

Mike says, slowly, "There are parts of your brain that are very scary."

"The frogs are for performance art purposes, by the way," Lisa says, eyebrows arched.

Freaky theater geeks. Mike doesn't mind them, but he doesn't think Lisa should date them. She's hot in this statuesque, down-home, country-spun, meat-and-potatoes way. "Larson would have no idea what to do with your boobs."

"Like you do?" Lisa shakes her head. "I need you to give up here," she says. "We'll be beffies, it'll be great, we can gossip about boys."

"I hate you." He sighs, because he very obviously doesn't hate Lisa.

"Whatever," Lisa says. "Grab the check. I don't want to miss the previews."

Friday late-nights at the Franklin 23 are insane. It's not the only movie theater in town, but it's the biggest, and it's directly behind the mall, so when all the stores start closing, everyone drifts westward.

It takes them twenty minutes to get through the ticket line, and Omar meets them at the snack bar with a bucket of popcorn and a blue raspberry Icee. He raises a mocking eyebrow at Mike.

"Save it," Mike says, cheeks heating.

"It's not that I don't enjoy talking about the possibility of

Jason being an alien, dude." Omar laughs. "Sometimes I even put you on speakerphone. The guys at the shop really get a kick out of it."

Mike groans. Omar is super cool, as far as his friends go. He's got a van, he plays a mean bass, and he gets along with pretty much everyone in the entire universe. There should be, like, tiny birds and woodland creatures following him around, only Mike is pretty sure Omar's dad, an avid outdoorsman, would just shoot and eat them. Anyway, Mike should probably take it easy with the weed.

Lisa pokes his back. "I want Skittles," she says.

"How can you still be hungry?" Mike asks.

"I'm not," she says. "Skittles don't count as food, duh."

Mike opens his mouth to argue that Skittles are part of the four main food groups—candy, cheese, cookies, and hamburgers—but she palms the side of his face and says, "Skittles, Michael. Line number three is moving pretty fast."

Mike grumbles, but does what she says. He's pretty whipped, he acknowledges this, and it's doubly sad now that apparently she's not even his girlfriend. Cam's gonna laugh his ass off.

By the time he gets to the counter, Mike's decided to get himself an Icee, too, and water for Lisa, and a pack of Goobers, and he says, "I'll have—" just as he looks up at the douche at the register. "Aw, hell."

He's gonna have to strangle Lisa later. Such a shame; she had a rich and fulfilling life ahead of her.

"Tate," the cashier says. He's got this gleam in his blue eyes, like Mike being alive is just hilarious.

Rook Wallace is evil. Too bad no one will believe Mike.

"Wallace," Mike says tightly. He needs to learn how to kill people with his mind. No messy fingerprints, and Wallace would be out of his life forever. That would be pretty sweet.

Wallace says, "What can I get you?" with this massive, sparkling smile, and it takes Mike a second to remember how to talk.

"Skittles," Mike says finally.

Wallace cocks his head while ringing him up. "That it?"

Mike nods. "Yeah."

When he's walking away, he totally kicks himself for being a pussy and forgetting his Goobers. He'll just steal Omar's Icee, and Lisa can suck it up—she didn't specifically *ask* for water.

Lisa pouts anyway when he hands over her candy.

"You're sharing," he says. "I had to talk to *Wallace.*"

"I like Wallace," Omar says, like he could ever hate anyone anyway. Mike has legitimately never even seen Omar get *angry* with anyone, even that time Meckles sat on his bass.

Mike points at him and says, "That's because he isn't after *your* soul." The bitch of it is that Wallace is a nice guy. Hell, he's even friendly with Jason, and Jason's a massive tool. Mike just happens to rightly believe that Wallace is the spawn of the devil, because no one knows how Wallace used to beat the crap out of him after Little League games when they were twelve. And no one will *ever* know. There's no way Mike is going to bring that up now; how embarrassing would that be?

Lisa ignores him and says, "Are we waiting for Meckles and Cam?"

Mike waves across the packed lobby toward Meckles. If his flaming red hair hadn't made him stand out, everything else about Meckles would have. Over six feet of solid muscle, currently making his way over to them in too much flannel and baggy jeans, like he time-traveled to modern-day Morrison from Seattle circa 1995. Mike would be ashamed to be seen with him, but Mike's an upstanding and giving guy. Plus, it's not like Cam's any better with his floral prints and his cargo shorts that he insists on wearing at least eleven months out of the year. He just pulls his socks up to his knees when he gets cold.

"Dudes," Meckles says. He bumps fists with Omar.

"Where's Cam?" Lisa asks.

"With Deanna." He makes a face. Meckles is thoroughly weirded out about Cam dating Deanna, mainly because she's Meckles' twin sister.

Mike approves, because Deanna is totally hot.

"Movie, guys, let's go," Omar says, jerking his head toward the ushers.

"No Jay?" Meckles asks.

"Damn it," Mike says. "Did anyone even call Jason?"

Omar waggles his cell phone in the air before tucking it into his back pocket. "He's babysitting, he'll meet us later. Now let's go before all the good seats are taken. I'm not sitting by myself again. Or with Meckles."

"Hey," Meckles says.

Omar hugs the bucket to his chest and says, "You touch my popcorn, you die."

When the movie lets out, they hang in the dimly lit side exit until security chases them off.

Lisa leans into Mike's side and loops their arms together, watching Meckles charge into Omar, flip him over his shoulder, and take off toward Omar's van. Omar isn't a little dude. He's smaller than Meckles—*everyone* is smaller than Meckles—but it's still pretty impressive.

"Huh," Mike says.

"What?" Lisa asks.

"Nothing." It's kind of chilly, so Mike twists his arm out of her grip and wraps it around her waist instead, pulling her closer, and wonders if it's okay to still hold her like this. "Just. Larson Kemp? Really?"

Lisa shrugs. "His accent's sexy. Plus, I'm thinking about joining drama, beef up my transcripts. I need to get more involved with school activities if I want to get into a good college."

Mike sighs. Really, it's a little tragic, all those estranged years between them. He thinks their relationship might've been more fulfilling if they hadn't needed sucking face as a reason to hang out. It's kind of messed up, now that he thinks about it. And mostly proves that one or both of them have some emotional issues. Ugh.

He's not even really *hurt* about Lisa's decision; his ego's bruised more than anything else. That probably says a lot about what was really going on.

At the van, Omar calls back to them, "Yo, we're meeting Jay at the Lot!"

Lisa nudges their hips together. She says, "I've realized a few things in the past couple weeks, you know," steering him across the parking lot toward Omar.

Mike turns his head, giving her a questioning look. "What?"

"Just"—she shakes her head—"some things." Her eyes are somber in the dim light spilling over the parking lot. There's no breeze, and her dark hair falls mostly straight and heavy around her face, bangs cutting just above her eyes. She looks like maybe she isn't as okay with their so-called breakup as she says she is, and Mike wants to know *why*. He kind of feels like he did something wrong, but he can't think of what that could be.

Mike seriously *hates* talking about feelings, though. He swallows back all his words and forces a shrug. "Okay."

• • •

The Lot is the stretch of cracked asphalt framing an abandoned Sears building at the rougher end of town—the Morrison ghetto, or what passes for a ghetto in suburbia. It's half lit by halogen spotlights—three of the five lights have been popped by douches with rocks, and it's not the kind of place where anyone would replace them. On the other end of the strip mall is a Payless and a Manhattan Bagel, but neither is open this late.

Cam and Deanna are sitting on a speed bump. Deanna has one red Converse on her skateboard, rolling it back and forth, but mostly her attention is on Cam and Cam's mouth.

"Ugh, gross," Meckles says.

"Girl Meckles!" Mike shouts, swooping in and wrapping his arms around their necks, leaning into their faces.

"Get *off*," Cam yelps, laughing. He flails and knees Mike in the thigh and sends an elbow into his armpit, while Deanna slaps both her hands at his chest.

"Had to do it," Mike says, stumbling backward and grinning at their expressions—Deanna's eyes are bright, belying her frown. "Meckles was about to seizure."

Cam sticks his tongue out at him, because Cam is approximately five years old.

It's not that crowded at the Lot for a Friday night. A couple scattered groups, some guys on bikes down at one end, a bunch of girls smoking in front of the Sears entrance.

Lisa tugs Deanna to her feet and Mike snags Deanna's skateboard, pushing shakily off toward the center of the Lot.

Lisa yells, "Careful," after him, and he hears Omar groan and say, "He's gonna brain himself one of these days."

Like Mike is *anywhere near* as bad as Cam.

So, okay, it's true that he's got absolutely no sense of balance. There's a very real reason why Mike's own skateboard, a much-begged-for gift for his thirteenth birthday, is buried in the back of his bedroom closet.

He should probably *never* be on a skateboard, but he can't help himself. Whenever he sees Girl Meckles' board he goes for it, thinking maybe he'll become magically better at it, but it never works. Whatever. It's a flat surface, and he's got all four wheels on the ground, and he likes to live a little dangerously. He *did* grow up with Cam, after all. Almost all of Mike's bad decisions throughout the years can be blamed on Cam, despite him being his very best bro, and Omar's usually the voice of reason that Mike should always listen to. Of course, more often than not, he doesn't.

The stupidity of that is suddenly highlighted when one of the wheels catches on a piece of gravel. The snag probably would've hardly even shaken a normal person, but it pitches Mike forward into the asphalt right in front of four strangers, who are, Mike gleans from a passing glance midfall, all relatively hot and cool. Great.

Mike is bleeding from an elbow and his chin feels raw. He rolls over onto his back, the pavement damp against his T-shirt. He coughs a little, staring up at the sky, at stars blurry with fuzzy nimbuses. He can hear Cam hooting in the distance.

"Are you okay?" a guy asks, and Mike blinks up at him, red faced. There's a light behind the guy's head that makes his hair glow like an angel.

It's possible that Mike's hit his head, too. "Maybe?" He pushes himself up so he's leaning on stinging palms.

"Oh my god," one of the girls says. "That was hilarious." She snaps her gum, grinning.

"Thanks," Mike says dryly.

The guy says, "Here," and leans down to help Mike up. Mike starts to go a little dizzy as he gains his feet, and he appreciates the guy's strong grip. Head wound is definitely looking likely.

"I'm good," Mike says.

"Sure." The dude has a nice smile, now that Mike can properly see his face. There's a lip ring involved. Mike's impressed.

"Nice, uh." Mike catches himself just in time, because complimenting a guy on his grin, even with a few screws knocked loose, is pretty weird. He manages to end the comment with "shirt," because he's motherfucking smooth.

"For real?" another girl says, incredulous. She's got ridiculous, tiny pigtails on top of her head, so Mike doesn't feel like he has to explain himself to the likes of her.

Just when he's sure he's going to have to commit seppuku

to get out of this with even a shred of dignity intact, Deanna and Lisa wander over.

Deanna flips her board up, grabs it with one hand and tucks it under her arm. She frowns and says, "Mike, we don't need a trip to the hospital tonight, okay? Stick to walking."

Great, now Girl Meckles is berating him—like she has any business lecturing anyone, considering the shenanigans Cam gets into on a daily basis—in front of whoever these people are. It doesn't really matter, since they're not anyone he's ever going to know, but he still kind of wants to melt into the pavement.

Mike shrugs tightly and lets Lisa thread their fingers together. She swings their arms as they walk, and Mike tries to shake off the weird, fuzzy feeling in his head. When he glances at her, Lisa's staring at him, smiling a little.

"What?"

Lisa waggles her eyebrows. "Nothing."

"Yeah?" He's not buying it.

She laughs and ruffles his hair with her other hand. "You're adorable sometimes," she says.

"I'm adorable *always*," he says, even though he's still confused.

"Whatever. C'mon, Cam's trying to convince Meckles to build him a bike ramp out of old fencing."

"That'll end well," Mike says. Cam is nuts. Mike might

have, like, inner ear issues or something, but at least he doesn't attempt to jump lines of trash cans on his dirt bike and then act surprised when he ends up taking a header straight into a pile of garbage.

Anymore. Mike doesn't do that *anymore*.

Lisa nods. "It'll end fantastic, and then we can watch Deanna yell at him a lot."

"Hey." Mike lifts their twined hands and points off toward where Omar's van is. There's a pale guy loitering. He's like a ghost, with hair so light it blends into his skin. "Isn't that your boy?"

Lisa jerks her hand out of his and punches him in the middle of the spine and hisses, "Don't point, oh my god, are you *dumb*?"

"Ow," he says, twisting his back. He glares at her. "He's not even looking this way."

Lisa's cheeks are pink.

Mike sighs and tilts their heads close together. "Lisa Linnet Delany," Mike says in a low voice, "stop freaking out. Larson would be lucky just to breathe the same air as you. He'd probably wet himself if you said hi; you're totally in. Just remember that I'll hurt him if he ever does anything to make you cry."

Lisa makes a face. "He's over six and a half feet tall," she says.

"Are you calling me short?"

"No, I'm calling you average. I'm calling *him* freakishly tall and dreamy."

Mike flicks his gaze to Larson and then back to Lisa. She's got that weird smile on her face again, and it kind of makes Mike want to vomit. "I will accept this," he says finally. "I'll sic Meckles on him instead."

"Michael," she says, exasperated.

"Lisa," Mike says, echoing her tone, "let me have this. I'm imagining Meckles getting some sweet punches in before Larson suggests a danceoff."

Lisa bites her lower lip. "That would be kind of funny."

"Hell, yeah." He pushes her toward the van. "Now go talk to him about paper frogs and interpretive dance."

She kisses his cheek and says, "I hate you."

It's getting even colder. Mike can almost see his breath. In front of the Payless, he sits on the edge of the cracked sidewalk next to Jason, his thin wrists resting on bent knees. There are flyers plastered all over the telephone pole next to him, and Mike reads them absently—three lost and founds, a couple roommates wanted, reminders about South Morrison High intramural baseball and soccer, open mic at the Beanery, an old *Vote for Fitzsimmons and Smith* sticker.

Jason's humming something lame under his breath.

Mike jostles him with his elbow. "Dude."

Jason blushes. "You have no appreciation for the classics," he says.

"I have plenty," Mike says. The Lemonheads, that's a classic band. Peter Cetera, not so much. He shakes his head and says, "Chicago," in this sad, disappointed way that always gets Jason scrambling to make him proud. Mike has no idea how or why this reaction started, but it's almost as good a reason to keep Jason around as Casio management.

Jason pulls out his iPod and gives Mike one of the earbuds. "Fall Out Boy, Nada Surf, or Bleachers?" he asks.

"Nada Surf, man," Mike says, then flops back on the cement to stare up at the stars.

three.

Weekends for Mike are usually a whole lot of bumming around in his pajama pants. He has a part-time job at his uncle's cheese shop, but he tries to keep his schedule mostly during the week, after school, so working won't conflict with the long stretches of nothing—with a side of possible band practice—on Saturday and Sunday.

Mostly, he spends as much time as he can with his little sister, because she pretty much worships him, and that's always gratifying. Plus, it keeps his mom off his back for when he wants to actually do shit. Rosie drives him crazy sometimes, but she's a cool little dude. Occasionally Mike'll end up playing with Barbies, but for the most part they just make forts or race tracks for her Matchbox cars and hermit crabs, and Mike can deal with that.

"Mikey."

"Rosalinda," Mike says, snapping together another LEGO. They're building a castle, have been building a castle for over an hour; castle building is serious business. They have recommended directions, but really they're just making it as tall as possible.

"Sandwich is hungry," Rosie says.

Mike looks up at her, eyebrow arched. She's got her hands balled on her hips, short blond hair still spiked from all the mousse Mike had put in it earlier, only it's kind of flat on one side now. "He is?"

"Yep." Rosie nods. Sandwich is her latest imaginary friend. Before him there was Box Head, and before that, Poppy Carlos. Rosie routinely gets notes from her first grade teacher that tiptoe around the fact that she's certifiably *weird*.

"Should we find Mom?" Mike gets to his feet, swiping his palms on his thighs. He groans and twists his back, because he's been sitting in one position too long. He's extra sore from the night before, and he's gonna have some sick scabs on his arm.

Rosie purses her lips, like she's really thinking about it. "Only if you think she'll give us pizza."

Mom'll give them tuna salad sandwiches and applesauce. Mike weighs the pros and cons of leaving Mom out of the lunch equation. She'll probably be pissed that they didn't drag her out of her office to eat, and there's a chance she'll smell the Ellio's before it's even out of the oven, but Mike decides he's willing to risk it if Rosie is.

They're successfully stealthy—Mom must be in a writing groove. He hasn't heard a peep from her since midmorning, when she'd stumbled out, zombie-like, for a coffee refill.

He pops in a movie while they eat. It's *Return of the Jedi*, because there's no arguing Rosie out of the Ewoks, but at least she's off her *Wizard of Oz* kick. They're just finishing up, empty plates on the coffee table, when the doorbell rings.

Mike stares in the direction of the front door from the couch for a minute. He doesn't feel like getting up. Maybe they'll go away.

"Door, Mikey," Rosie says, eyes glued on the TV.

It rings again.

Mom yells, "Door, Michael," from the back of the house, so Mike heaves himself to his feet with a sigh.

On the other side of the door is a tiny black-haired girl with a huge smile and bangle bracelets all the way up to her elbows. There's glitter all over her cheeks. She says, "Hi!" and, "Can Rosie come out and play?"

Mike doesn't know how the Wallace family can produce such a strange spectrum of offspring. There's Rook, the jock-ified douche, then Serge, the pale-faced, basement-dweller *artiste*, Lilith, who Mike's never actually heard talk, at least not in English, and finally Teeny, who is probably not actually named Teeny, but Mike's never heard her called anything else.

Teeny Wallace is deep in the throes of puppy love with Rosie. It's funny, because it's kind of obvious Rosie doesn't actually know what to do with her. They don't have a lot in common, so of course, they're basically inseparable.

"Rosie's watching a movie," Mike says, then waits to see whether Teeny will invite herself in or not. It could go either way.

She fidgets on the stoop, shiny, mary-janed feet pressing on top of each other, right hand playing with the hem of her pink skirt.

Mike surreptitiously scouts the front yard for signs of Rook Wallace. They live four houses down, and it's theoretically possible that he's using his baby sister to lure Mike out of the house for a good old-fashioned beat-down. Not that that seems to be his style, nowadays. Wallace is apparently far too freaking *nice* to beat the ever-loving crap out of him anymore. Mike doesn't trust the peace. He doubts Wallace has had such a change of heart—more likely he's just biding his time. Probably. It's been a few years, but that doesn't mean Mike should just let his guard down. Wallace has been smiling at him a lot more lately, which probably means he's just waiting for the perfect time to eat all the flesh from his bones.

Teeny finally lets out a breathy sigh and says, "Okay," and then just stands there, staring up at him with her huge, baby deer eyes. She's *adorable*. He doesn't get how she can be related to Wallace.

Mike steps aside and says, "C'mon in," waving a hand toward the den.

Rosie doesn't acknowledge her beyond shifting over when Teeny drops to sit on the rug next to her.

Mike sighs. They're quiet now, but he knows sooner or later Teeny's going to make noise about playing house or bakery or Candy Land, and Rosie's going to say no. And then they're going to get into a screaming fight, complete with tears. Rosie will stomp upstairs and slam her bedroom door, and Teeny will make her way huffily home and come back an hour later with an entire sketchbook filled with these I'm-sorry drawings that Mike's pretty sure are supposed to be cats and teddy bears and ducks but basically all just look like dragons and weird cheese. This happens at least once a week.

Before anything like that can even start, though, Cam texts Mike: *practice @ meckles*

He pokes his head into his mom's office to let her know he's taking off, then heads out to meet the guys.

Mike drives his mom's car over to Meckles'. Since she basically works from home, it's easier to just use hers—on the rare occasions that he can't get Omar or Cam to swing by and pick him up—than it is to save up for a car of his own.

Band practice is always in Meckles' basement. It used to be in Meckles' garage, but then his dad started getting pissed off that he could never park his car inside, so they migrated, because they're easygoing dudes. Mike's not sure Meckles' dad is thrilled with them being under their kitchen either, but the most he does is complain about them leaving drinks on the felt of his pool table.

Mike says hi to Meckles' mom as he lets himself in the back door, and then he slinks down into the basement, guitar case hefted over his shoulder.

"Hey," he says when he hits the bottom of the stairs. It's muggy, and smells like feet and ass.

Jason is folded up on the floor, playing with something on the back of his keyboard. Meckles is absently tapping out a rhythm on his snare drum. Cam, a white, soft-brimmed cap mashing down his blond curls, is sprawled on the beaten, sagging couch, singing Bon Jovi.

"Are we really practicing today, or did you just call me over to fuck off?" Mike says. He drops his guitar case on Cam's stomach and Cam gives him a dirty look. "Where's Omar?"

"Here."

Mike bends down to peek under the pool table. Omar waves at him from the floor, where he's lying on his back, bass resting on his belly.

"So," Mike says, straightening back up, "fucking off, I can dig it."

Cam rolls his eyes. "Just get your shit set up."

Omar shimmies out and gets to his feet. He tugs the strap of his bass over his head and glances meaningfully at Mike, like he hasn't been wasting just as much time staring at the underside of the pool table.

Mike has never been able to successfully one-up Omar, though, so he just sighs and starts lugging the amps off of the far wall, unrolling all their wires.

"Oh, hey, check this out," Cam says, sitting up, "I came up with a sweet name for us."

"I'm vetoing anything that has the words *assclown* or *pussylicker* in it," Omar says absently. He's fiddling with his bass, humming occasionally under his breath.

Cam's face falls. Cam is nothing if not extremely predictable.

Mike turns to Meckles and says, "Seriously?" because Cam has an actual, real-life, totally cool girlfriend, and Mike has no idea how that happened. "You let your sister *date* that?"

"I don't *let* Deanna do anything," Meckles says, offended. "Have you seen her?"

Deanna has Meckles' height, half a foot taller than Cam, and she's gorgeous and boy-hipped. She also shaves the sides of her head in the summer and designs most of her own clothes, held together by safety pins instead of thread.

"She's scary," Cam says with a dreamy smile.

Jason plays the opening notes to "Axel F" on his keyboard. Mike'll never admit it out loud, but Jason is occasionally his favorite.

• • •

"What's up with you and Lisa?" Omar asks. He's caught Mike outside, sitting on the edge of the Meckleses' concrete patio, smoking a cigarette. It's spitting out, a fine, soaking mist, but there's an awning, so only Mike's sneakers are getting wet.

"Nothing," Mike says.

Omar pretty much has zero bad habits, because Omar is awesome. Mike's mom calls him a good influence. He's squeaky clean, almost to the point of nerd. Like Jason, if Jason had a shaved head and looked as super fly in sunglasses. Mike kind of wants to be Omar when he grows up.

"That's what I meant," Omar says.

Mike shrugs. "We're fine."

"Right," Omar says, like he doesn't believe him. "Cam says you broke up."

"Yeah, well." Mike deflates; the *Cam's a bitch* is silent but there. "Maybe."

Omar makes a sympathetic sound and swings an arm over Mike's shoulders.

Mike's starting to feel like a girl here, but he leans into Omar anyway.

"Apparently we weren't really dating, though," Mike feels compelled to say. The weight of the words could go either way—he's kind of upset that Lisa hadn't been taking him seriously, but also relieved that nothing got messy, that apparently there wasn't anything there to get messy *about*.

Omar doesn't agree or disagree, which Mike appreciates.

He just says, "Okay," and then shoves Mike off the edge of the patio. "Come on, Mom Meckles is making sandwiches."

Later that night, holed up in his room, Mike makes a list. A list to make himself feel better and to organize his thoughts, which he does sometimes. No one knows about his lists, because Cam would laugh his ass off and Jason would want to start talking about *feelings*, like the gigantic dork he is. Mike's lists are private.

So he makes a pro and con list about the breakup, and sees that the pros far outweigh the cons: 1. He can hook up with other people. 2. He still gets to hang out with Lisa. 3. He'll save money. 4. He doesn't have to do whatever she says (although, who is he kidding, he'll probably do whatever she says *anyway*).

The con side mainly consists of really, really, really hating asking girls out. He doesn't actually *want* to date. He's been through that already. It's mostly psychologically painful, and the mutual groping is—okay, it's damn well worth it, he's a guy, but it's still awkward as fuck sometimes. That's why the thing with Lisa had been so convenient, but even Mike thinks that's a lousy reason to stay together. Or, like, beg Lisa to take him back.

Lisa would just make sad faces and then kick him in the balls.

Mike flops back on his bed and stares at his ceiling. This

all would've made more sense, he thinks, if Lisa'd had any actual contact with Larson before this. As far as Mike knows, they don't even have any classes together.

He sighs, closes his eyes, and then pops them open again when he feels a weight dip the edge of his bed. Rosie is staring at him, wearing her favorite pair of Teenage Mutant Ninja Turtles pajamas. The kid's got the *stealth* of a ninja. She also has Godzilla's shell in her fist, and the poor little guy has all his legs out, searching for land.

She says, "I can't find Professor Cheese," and her eyes are red and watery. It's the fifth time Professor Cheese has gotten out of the aquarium and they *always* find him, but Rosie has a strange and strong attachment to her hermit crabs, since Mom won't let them get a dog. Mom's written three books: *Professor Cheese's Great Escape, Professor Cheese and the Unhelpful House Mouse*, and *Professor Cheese Is Scared of the Dark!* Sometimes Mike thinks the only reason she had kids was for inspiration.

"He'll turn up," Mike says, but Rosie looks like she's either going to start wailing or hitting him in the arm with her fist—she's got some power when she's all wound up.

"Michael." He glances over at his doorway where his mom is leaning tiredly against the frame. She has her ratty bathrobe pulled on over her nightgown, and a thick headband is holding her hair off her face, so Rosie must've gotten her out of bed, too. She's frowning at him, like maybe she doesn't already know he's going to help. Like he actually *wouldn't*, with both of them looking at him like that.

He sighs and says, "Put 'Zilla away and we'll go look around the kitchen." Twice, they've found him on his way out to the back porch.

As Mike crawls around the hard tile floor, calling for the Professor, he thinks about how all the women in his life seriously suck, and how he can't seem to say no to any of them.

four.

Lisa joins drama on Monday.

Also on Monday, Mike gets tricked into joining SMH intramural baseball. Although, not exactly tricked, but Theo
Higgins asked him, and nobody ever says no to Theo Higgins. Well, Lisa does—he's been asking her out at least once
a week since freshman year—but Mike has never been able
to. He's got these huge eyes and he's basically perfect and
adorable and pocket-sized. He's *wee*. He also kicks really
hard and used to steal Mike's lunch money all through elementary school, but that's beside the point.

Anyway, he said yes, and he expects it to all be very *High
School Musical 2*, considering the crowd of dancers Higgins
normally hangs with. Naturally, Mike expects his friends
to play, too.

And, okay, Mike does have some athletic experience. His
and Cam's Little League baseball team, the Lowell's Hard-
ware Cougars, went to state two years in a row, and he knows
he's still got a strong swing. He'd actually thought about
trying out for the high school junior varsity team freshman year, and even made it all the way onto the practice

fields, but then Wallace, former star pitcher for the Scalzetti Assorted Meats Rams—and the Cougars' biggest rivals—had shown up, and Mike didn't want to deal with that. He'd slipped out of tryouts without looking back.

At least Wallace won't be anywhere near him this time, since varsity players aren't allowed to participate.

There's a farm park across the street from the high school, with a four-mile path that winds through woods and cornfields and rented vegetable gardens. The track and field team uses it every day for practice. In the afternoon, while waiting for Cam to get out of detention, Mike and Meckles lounge in the grass by the park's tiny gravel parking lot, giving Jason crap for whatever he's doing that day—sprinting, long jumps, baton twirling—which he apparently has to wear these amazingly tiny shorts for.

Jason isn't really all that tall—he's shorter than Mike—but he's mostly skin and bones, with long, lean legs, so he manages to look like a freaky praying mantis, anyway.

"Bones with sleeves!" Meckles yells as Jason runs past, and Mike stifles a laugh with the side of his wrist, because Meckles is *lame*, what the hell, but that's still funny as shit.

Jason flips them off. He's learning. Before joining their unnamed band of awesomeness he'd been an emo loser who wrote bad poetry and listened to M83 in the dark. Probably. Mike may be assuming a little here, but he's sure there was a terrifying amount of loneliness that Mike has since saved him from. Mike's cool like that.

Mike knocks his elbow into Meckles and says, "We're playing intramural baseball. Starts next week."

"What?" Meckles goes pale—he has a pathological fear of organized sports.

Mike grins at him. "I signed you up. I'm not doing that shit alone." He'd also signed up Cam and Omar, but they won't care.

Meckles looks like he's going to have a heart attack. *"What?"* he says again, only with his hand clutching his chest.

Mike thinks it's hysterical. "Don't worry, we can get drunk first."

"No we can't," Meckles says. "I'll throw up. We'll all throw up, it'll be anarchy."

"I don't know, I think it'll be pretty cool," Mike says.

"What'll be cool?" Lisa says, dropping down on the grass next to Mike. Her book bag hits Mike in the shoulder, and Mike stares at her.

"What the hell are you *wearing*?" he asks, ignoring her question. Lisa has some sort of butt-ugly vest on over her T-shirt. There are hideous buttons of varying shapes and sizes all down the front.

She straightens up and smiles at him, tugging on the ends of the vest. "Larson made it for me. It's macramé."

"It's—I don't even know, it's like you let Meckles throw up all over you," Mike says. He tilts his head. With the sun shining on it, it looks like it's made out of every possible shade of puke brown imaginable.

Lisa ignores him and narrows her eyes at Meckles. "You *do* look like you're going to hurl. What's up?"

"Intramural baseball," Meckles says weakly.

Lisa continues to look confused.

Mike says, "You realize that Meckles hasn't participated in gym for over two years, right?"

"How is that even possible?"

"I had a panic attack once. Mr. Farragut thought I was dying. He lets me run laps instead of playing—" Meckles cuts off, like he can't say the actual words out loud, and ends up miming with wiggly fingers.

Mike says, "Is that supposed to mean organized sports? Because it looks like a puppet show about explosions and gay sex. Or jazz hands, which is basically the same thing."

Lisa makes a choking sound, hand over her mouth, eyes dancing.

Mike claps Meckles on the back. "Man up, dude."

Meckles says, "If I keel over and die it'll be all your fault."

"No one's ever died from a little friendly competition," Lisa says, smiling.

Meckles doesn't look convinced. Mike can't wait until he gets him out on the diamond. He knows there's no way Meckles will actually *play*, but it'll totally be funny trying to make him.

• • •

Mike wakes up with his face mashed into Cam's rug. His eyes are gummy and there's a crusty film trailing away from his mouth from dried drool. He groans as he rolls over to blink up at the ceiling. Something not good is happening inside his body.

Then the door bangs open and Cam's brother, Zack, says, "Rise and shine, chuckleheads," and Mike winces and tries not to throw up all over himself.

What the hell *happened* last night?

"Come on, princess." Zack nudges Mike with the toe of his sneaker. "You'll be late for school."

There's a crash, and then Mike hears Cam say something about his liver and death and eating Zack's face off.

Zack just laughs and flicks on the overhead light.

"You're dead to me," Mike says, tossing an arm over his eyes. When his brain stops trying to ooze out of his skull, he thinks back to the night before. He remembers following Cam home after his detention and finding a note Cam's dad left saying he was working late along with a twenty for pizza. He remembers—he makes a face—he remembers Natty Light and Vladimir vodka. He always forgets how truly shitty he feels after cheap alcohol. Zack is such an asshole for corrupting minors, and on a school night, too. At least he's pretty sure he called his mom to tell her he was sleeping at Cam's before Zack cracked open the liquor. He doesn't have a curfew, but he can really only get away with this during the week if he's staying with the Scotts.

Mike practically crawls down the stairs and into the kitchen, where Cam and Zack's dad is making bacon, because Cam and Zack's dad is awesome.

Mike's dad is not a real person. Or, well, obviously he's a real person; it's probably more accurate to say Mike's biological dad is not a real dad. He's a sperm donor. And not in the derogatory, absentee father way, but in the actual anonymous sperm donor way, as in how Mike's mom is a single, professional woman who happened to want babies. Mike is pretty okay with this.

It helps that Cam and Zack's dad had some sort of cosmic-sibling-slash-best-friend insta-bond with Mike's mom after they first met, back when Cam and Mike were in preschool. Now he's Mike's honorary uncle "Jem," a mangled form of James that only Mike's allowed to use— only fair, since Cam's called Mike's mom Al since they were six and he had trouble with just about every syllable of Allison.

Zack sits down at the breakfast bar with a mug of coffee, smirking at him. He looks coolly put together for someone who did at least four shots of vodka with them last night. There are no shadows under his eyes, and his back and shoulders are straight under his work polo. He looks clean-cut and handsome and not at all like someone who had dared Mike to, if he remembers correctly, down all those expired wine coolers. Yuck.

Mike would glare at him, but he doesn't think his head

could take it. Instead, he just reaches over and swipes Zack's coffee.

Zack doesn't put up much of a fight, though, because despite being a cheery, asshole morning person, he's inherited most of the other awesome Scott genes that seem to have skipped Cam completely. He's usually one of Mike's very favorite people.

Uncle Jem raises an eyebrow at Mike, but thankfully doesn't comment on his obvious hangover. He just slides a plate of crispy, greasy, delicious bacon his way. If only he knew how much alcohol Zack had bought for them.

Cam shuffles in, groaning like a zombie, and Uncle Jem wordlessly pours him a large glass of orange juice.

"You're a god among men, Pop," Cam says. After downing the whole thing, his eyes are almost fully open.

One corner of Uncle Jem's mouth curves up. He says, "First bell is in fifteen minutes, and I'm not writing you a note."

"Shit," Cam says.

They're both wearing the same clothes they wore the day before. Mike runs a hand through his scruffy, dirty-blond hair and says, "Fuck it, let's go."

Mike is almost 99 percent certain Meckles carried him to his second period class. He wakes up with a start when Mrs. Saunders slaps her copy of *Hamlet* on the edge of his desk, and he could have sworn Dougherty had been shoving theorems down his throat only minutes before.

Mike presses his palms into his dry eye sockets.

Someone chuckles, and Mike glares blearily over at Wallace. Because Meckles apparently dropped him off right in the front row next to *Wallace*. Awesome.

Meckles is dead to him. He mouths *You're dead to me* across the room to where Meckles is grinning smugly by the windows. Meckles, Zack, that lunch lady who refuses to save him the fresh soft pretzels from A lunch: all dead.

"You look like shit," Wallace says, grinning like this is making his entire day.

Mike grunts, trying not to think about the fact that Meckles probably hefted him down the hall in a fireman's carry. That's only slightly less embarrassing than being cradled bridal style.

This day just keeps getting better.

Normally, Mike sits in the back of English with Mo Howard. Meckles never sits with him, because Meckles is in love with Mrs. Saunders, and he likes to be up front where he can raise his hand as much as possible and gaze at her with these giant moon eyes—even though he says it's because he likes *English*. This could be true, given that Meckles has trouble speaking to anyone of the opposite gender besides his sister and Lisa, and even Lisa's iffy.

Mike twists around in his chair to search out Mo. They've done many an English project together—solid C work, and

Mike doesn't complain. Mo gives him a questioning look, gesturing toward Wallace, and Mike gives her a half shrug. He has no idea why Wallace isn't complaining about him sitting there, either.

He's kind of waiting for Chris Leoni to kick his ass for being in his seat, too, but all that happens is Wallace thunks a bottle of water down in front of him and says, "Drink this."

"Why, is it poisoned?"

Wallace looks at him funny. "No."

Mike isn't convinced. "Did you spit in it?"

"A little spit won't kill you," Wallace says. At Mike's frown, he rolls his eyes. "It's not even opened, Tate. Just drink the damn water."

Mike sullenly twists the cap off, breaking the seal, and takes a sip. When he tries to give the bottle back, Wallace shakes dark hair out of his eyes and says, "Keep it."

Mike kind of wants to peg the bottle at Wallace's head, but the sad fact is that water is delicious, and when Wallace brandishes a tiny Advil container, Mike starts seriously considering making declarations of love and marriage. It's pathetic, Mike's ashamed of himself, even as he says, "Gimme," and wrestles the Advil out of Wallace's hands.

"You're welcome," Wallace says, amused.

Mike says, "If I die later, everyone will know it was you."

• • •

"This just in," Cam says at lunch, sitting down next to Deanna and dropping an arm across her shoulders, "I'm the coolest."

Mike flips him the finger. "Why does this week suck so hard?"

"Because you think listening to Cam is a valid life choice," Lisa says.

Cam points at himself and says, "Coolest."

"Wallace keeps smirking at me," Mike says. He's totally not whining; he's just frustrated. Wallace has this complete asshole-ish look that he gives Mike when nobody else is watching. Like Mike owes him all his unborn children for three measly tabs of Advil. Like Wallace is really going to *enjoy* collecting all his unborn children.

"Mo Howard said you were all over Wallace in English," Cam says. He mimes giving a blow job and Mike really wants to punch him.

Instead, Mike goes completely red and says, "Shut up."

Lisa pats his arm. "It's okay, Michael," she says soothingly, and Mike doesn't bother asking her *what's* okay, because he's not sure he actually wants to know.

five.

On the second Saturday in September,
Mike wakes up to Lisa leaning over him, long dark hair
sweeping forward, shading her face like some sort of death
wraith, only with pretty eyes. His mom must have let her
in. It's happened before, but it's doubly annoying now that
they're not dating anymore.

"Two words for you, Tate," she says, poking him in the
ribs. "Student council."

Mike rubs both his hands over his face and yawns noisily. "What?"

"Student council. I want to be our class president."

Mike knows Lisa is saying actual words, but they're not
making any coherent sense. "What? Since when do you care
about our class?"

Lisa moves to the edge of the bed as Mike struggles into
a sitting position, propping his back up against the wall.
"Since I looked over all my college applications," she says. She
ticks off her fingers. "St. Mary's, NYU, Duke, Georgetown,
they're looking for well-rounded straight-A students. All I've
got right now is Honor Society and drama."

Mike stares at her. She looks pretty serious. "Okay," he says. He's still not sure why she had to wake him up with this information at—he glances at the clock—nine thirty in the morning. He'd been up until three with Cam. This is *way* too early.

Lisa says, "You need to be my running mate."

Mike laughs. "You're on crack, no way am I running for *vice president*," he says.

"You have to!" she says. "We can sell you as gay, it'll be edgy."

Seriously, they're *real words*, he's pretty sure of that, but it's all gobbledygook to Mike. He pinches the bridge of his nose. "But I'm not gay. And even if I *were* gay, I wouldn't be campaigning with it."

Lisa arches an eyebrow. "C'mon, Mike."

Mike drops his hand onto his lap. "What?"

She leans in close again, their foreheads almost touching. "Michael," she says meaningfully. Her eyebrows are pretty much all the way up under her bangs.

"What?" He's not *gay*. You can totally admire another dude's shoulders or legs or *shirt* and not be gay. So he thinks Zack's a good-looking guy. So what?

"It's cool to be gay," Lisa says.

"It's not cool to be gay. It's kind of cool to *act* gay." He knows this. Every time Cam gets up in Mike's space during shows with the band—which, let's face it, have only happened during house parties in Cam's massive backyard—all the girls scream. It'd be embarrassing if it wasn't sort of amazing instead. "Or it's cool to be gay in theory. Or it's cool to be bi, in the sense that you date girls, but girls can imagine you making out with other guys if they want."

Lisa makes a face.

"Yeah, see," Mike says. "Not actually cool."

She gives him a skeptical look. "So you're freaking out."

"No! There's no freaking out here. Nothing to be freaked out *about*." He thumbs his chest. "Not gay."

She gets a shrewd, mean gleam in her eyes, like maybe she's about to take down a baby antelope. Mike's seen this look before, but usually it's aimed at Cam or Theo Higgins. "Says the dude who made out with Junior Meat King."

Mike freezes. Like every molecule in his body just went terrified. He makes a *What?* sound, but his throat is kind of stuck closed.

"You and the little sausage man, remember?" She crosses her arms over her chest, smug. "Last month at Cam's end of the summer blowout. Full-on making out, with tongues, and hands in private places." Her eyes go hazy and she licks her lips. *Gross.*

"No way," Mike manages. Josh Jacob Scalzetti, son of the Butcher of Morrison? "No fucking way." Granted, he doesn't really remember much of that night, but he sure as hell would've remembered *that*, right?

Lisa eyes him askance, a small smile curling the corners

of her mouth. "Are you more upset that you made out with J. J., or that you made out with a boy?"

Mike ignores her, palming his face in utter shame. J. J. goes to Catholic school across town, thank God, but—"Who else saw this?"

"Uh, everybody?"

Which is a lie, because if Meckles or Cam saw that shit, it wouldn't have taken this long to get back to him. Mike slides his hand down to cover his mouth and stares at her.

Lisa throws up her arms. "Fine. A bunch of girls from Our Lady, Rook, me, Jason—"

"*Jason?*" Mike says. Then, "Wait, *Wallace?*" Fuck. He pulls the covers up over his head and groans, burrowing back down into his bed. "Kill me."

"It's not a big deal," she says. "Just saying, you shouldn't be so quick to dismiss the bi thing, you know, you looked like you were having fun."

Mike rips the covers back, bolts upright again, and says, "J. J.'s an *asshole!*" J. J.'s a slick, pansy-ass *preppy*. He wears sweater vests and ties and khakis even when he's *not* in school. There are fraternization rules, and Mike broke about fifty of them. Oh god, his *tongue* had been in J. J.'s *mouth*.

"I like what you're focusing on here," Lisa says, nodding.

"Why was he even at Cam's?"

Lisa sighs. "It was a party, Michael, I'm pretty sure *everyone* was there."

"And also—also, why are you just telling me this now? That was over three weeks ago."

"That's really not important," Lisa says, visibly exasperated now. She's probably annoyed that they're off topic, but seriously. *Seriously.*

"Are you kidding me? Up until last week you were my *girlfriend.* Oh shit, Lisa, everyone thinks I'm gay, don't they?" This explains why Wallace has been extra-specially evil since school started. Usually he's just an asshole to Mike behind everyone's back—they think he's so nice and sweet and thoughtful, when really he's just a giant, back-stabbing poser—but lately he's been a *smirky* asshole. No wonder.

"I told you, it's not a big deal," Lisa says.

Mike pushes back the blankets and swings his legs over the side of the mattress. "I don't know." It looks like the end of the world from where Mike's sitting. If he squints a little.

"Okay, look. *Look,*" Lisa says. She slides onto her feet, stands in between his knees and places her hands on his shoulders. "It's done. Now, Mike—now, you've got to own it."

Mike says, slowly, "Own it."

"Yeah. Own your gayness," she says. "And then run for student council with me."

Mike doesn't know if he can own something he isn't sure how he got, or if it's even his. What if J. J. took advantage of a hot-sexy babe hallucination? But at this point he'll look like a douche trying to deny it. "Can we just . . . not talk about it ever again?"

Lisa shrugs. "We could try."

Mike falls back and stares up at his bare ceiling. "Fine."

It isn't until later that Mike realizes the greater implication. Not that he's made out with a guy, with *J. J.*, of all douche bags, but that he'd been dating *Lisa* at the time. He gropes for his cell on his bedside table and calls Lisa and says, "Did you break up with me because I cheated on you?" as soon as she picks up.

There's some ominous silence. And then, "Mike?"

"Shit," Mike says, because that's Karin answering Lisa's phone, and Lisa's older sister is frightening. She used to be really good at making Mike eat mud. He yelps, "I'm gay!" and hangs up, and Lisa calls him back five minutes later, laughing her ass off.

She can't even make coherent conversation. Mike stays on the line for all of it, even when he hears Karin cackling in the background, because this whole mess is his own damn fault. At least neither one of them appears to be gearing up to kick him in the balls. This is a good thing.

Finally, she says, "I didn't break up with you because you cheated on me, Mike, geez. We weren't even dating."

Mike doesn't really see it that way, but whatever. He sighs. "I can't believe you waited so long to bring this up. You knew I didn't remember anything."

Lisa says, "Mostly."

She *totally* knew he didn't remember the whole J. J. thing. There is no way she would have respected his boundaries about that.

"I was waiting to use it on something really good," Lisa admits.

"Like blackmail."

"Or not," Lisa says. "I just wanted to savor the look on your face."

"Lisa—"

"Do you not remember flirting with that guy at the Lot? Or the way you stare at Zack's ass, like, all the time?"

"You lie, I do not," Mike says. Zack has a good ass, that's a totally objective observation. How did this conversation get so out of control?

Lisa sighs. She says, "Look, Mike," then pauses, and Mike can picture her rubbing her forehead, her eyes closed. "Look. I'd rather just be your friend, okay? And I really *do* like Larson. And you have some issues to work out." She sounds resigned, but not unhappy.

"Okay," Mike says, drawn out, still not entirely clear on everything Lisa is and is not saying.

"You are, however," Lisa says cheerfully, "running for VP in order to make up for breaking my fragile female heart."

Mike says, "Bullshit," but he's got little to no conviction in his voice.

"You're the best friend a gal can have," she says.

Mike's life is fucked up. He rolls his eyes up to his ceiling and makes a big decision. A huge, important decision, because he figures otherwise he might go crazy.

"I'm going clean for a while," Mike says. "I need a clear head to figure this all out."

Lisa makes a weird sound.

"What?" Mike says, defensive. He can be sober. He doesn't *have* to get high. Or listen to Cam.

Lisa says, "I'm pretty sure that's the most intelligent thing you've ever said."

"I'm hanging up now," Mike says.

Lisa makes kissy noises and hangs up first.

"I am completely whipped," Mike says, heaving his messenger bag onto the lab table.

"By everyone, it's pathetic," Omar says absently, pulling out his chemistry book.

He'd argue that, but it's so true. Adults, kids, guys, girls, hermit crabs . . . Mike is a ginormous pushover. He sees this now with crystal clarity. He slumps into his seat next to Omar and sighs.

Omar looks over at him curiously. "That's not necessarily a bad thing, you know," he says.

Mike blinks at him. "You just called me pathetic."

"All right," Omar smiles, "more like endearing."

"Dumb," Mike says. He stares morosely down at the chipped black tabletop. "So fucking dumb."

"I'll say."

Mike jumps a little when Wallace's hip hits the side of their table. *Jesus.*

"Good picture of you, though," Wallace says, holding one of the class election flyers Lisa's been spreading around. He smiles with half his mouth. It's Wallace's charming, self-deprecating smile that always makes Lisa—*Lisa,* who makes distasteful noises around *kittens,* because she clearly has the soul of a hardened Viking—sort of all-around melty.

Mike is immune. He opens his mouth for a snappy, if not exactly witty comeback when it suddenly hits him that Wallace—his archnemesis, Rook motherfucking Wallace— has seen him *suck face with J. J. Scalzetti.*

Wallace's brow furrows. "You okay? You just went— white."

Omar jostles his arm. "Mike?"

Mike weighs the odds of getting sick all over the Bunsen burner if he tries to answer him. Finally, he manages a raspy "Fine."

He is so fucked.

"I hope you're happy," Mike says to Lisa. They're in the magazine room of the school library. It's empty except for them, a stack of flyers, and half a dozen pieces of poster board.

"Ecstatic," she says. She's putting the finishing touches on her election speech, so she isn't really paying much attention to Mike, who is steadily but surely going insane. "Why am I happy again?"

"This! This whole—" Mike spreads his arms, flaps them a little, like maybe he can express the exact magnitude of shit his life has dive-bombed into with his meager wingspan.

"You better not be implying I made you gay," she says, eyes narrowed.

"No, apparently the *Junior Meat King* made me gay," Mike says.

Lisa heaves a sigh and closes her laptop in a deliberate, put-upon motion. "Mike. You're freaking out."

Mike reaches up, digs his hands into his hair. "Is there any reason why I *shouldn't* be freaking out?" He hooked up with a dude. *Wallace* saw him hooking up with a dude, and Wallace may be a *nice guy*, but Mike isn't really counting on that lasting—there is absolutely no reason for Wallace to keep this to himself, right? Just because he hasn't said anything *yet*, doesn't mean he's going to stay quiet about it for forever. Right?

"I need to get this done," Lisa says, flicking her pen at him. "Seriously, it'll be fine. Stop worrying about it."

Mike doesn't see how he *can* stop worrying about it, because so far all that Mike has realized in his quest for sober findings is that dicks freak him out—not his own, obviously—and that all the gay porn he found is *scary*. Add to that a smug, smirking Wallace and Mike wants to bury himself in a hole for the rest of the school year. He doesn't want people staring at him, wondering. He doesn't want anyone talking about him behind his back.

"I don't think I can own this," Mike says, slumping down in the seat across from Lisa. He's pretty sure he can't even borrow it.

"Okay."

"Okay?"

"I'm not going to push you into something you don't want," Lisa says.

Mike glances pointedly at his mug plastered on VP flyers.

Lisa rolls her eyes. "Not with anything important," she says. "I think it'd be good for you, to try this, but you don't *have* to, nobody's making you. You can go for Mo Howard instead. She's got a crush on you the size of a small planet."

Mike makes a face at the lacquered wood of the table. *Cameron Scott is a giant man-whore* is carved into it, blue pen scratched into the grooves, and Mike traces it with his thumbnail. Mo's cute. She's small and adorable and has at least five piercings in her face, but Mike isn't honestly attracted to her outside her ability to rock iambic pentameter and the way she's always up for using silly voices whenever they have to act out a scene in a play.

"Whatever," Mike says. He face-plants onto the table, forehead pillowed by his arms. "I hate my life."

six.

Intramural baseball is basically just six
weeks of after-school pickup games on the Little League
diamond at the community center, since it's left empty
for the fall.

On the first day, Meckles panics and accidentally
punches Theo Higgins in the stomach and it's the single
funniest thing Mike has ever seen. Meckles spends a half
hour hyperventilating into a paper bag, and when Higgins
finally picks himself off the ground he kicks Meckles off
the playing field, so no real harm done. Meckles hadn't even
hit him that hard, Higgins just had to be a bitch about it.

As a team captain, Mike picks Cam, Omar—even though
Omar, despite his awesomeness at everything else, sucks at
baseball—and Mo before Higgins can get his grubby little
paws on her, since Mo still plays in a softball summer league
and isn't afraid to get dirty. Mike doesn't think Higgins
knows that, though. She's Mike's secret weapon. He also
picks Dotty—who's only there because Mo dragged her—
over Weedy Jim, who Mike's pretty sure has asthma. Turns
out, Dotty can run.

Officially, Mike's team is the Blue team, but unofficially he's calling them the Bobcats, because it sounds cool, and Dotty says she can make them T-shirts.

He's calling Higgins' team the Slugs; he's hoping it'll catch on.

The evening is cool, but Mike ends up a sweaty mess anyway by the time they wrap up. He's got dirt rash down the outside of his right arm, and there's a throb in his ankle from a slide toward home, but he's grinning. He'd forgotten how much he loves this.

Swinging an arm over Cam's shoulder, he says, "Good times, Cam. Good times." Cam and Mike seriously used to rule the diamond, little jocks in training. Mike doesn't know what happened to them, but he's glad they didn't end up super douches like Wallace and Chris Leoni.

"The Slugs are going down," Cam says happily, punching his fist into his glove. "Six weeks, twelve games. I don't even think Jim actually knows how to play. This is gonna be easy, even with the suckage fest that is Omar Hudson on our side."

Omar tucks his glove into his backpack. "Thanks, Cam."

"We should dress Meckles up like a bobcat," Cam says. "He can be our mascot."

"Good game," Higgins says with a half sneer as they walk past him. Mike wants to claw at his face, but he also kind of wants to give him a hug. Higgins sneering is like a puppy having a beef with its own tail. His brown hair flops over his forehead and he blows out of the corner of his mouth to get it away from his eyes. It doesn't work, and he finally just shoves a marginally clean part of his arm up and over his head, sweat slicking it back, and Mike had never really noticed how perfectly proportioned his nose is, and how red his bottom lip is, like he's been biting at it, and *Mike is in so much trouble, Jesus Christ.*

Mike clears his throat and turns to stare pointedly at the nearly deserted parking lot. He hates Lisa. She could've just not said anything ever, and maybe then life would've been kind enough to leave him with his heterosexual delusions. He could've found happiness in a vagina. Hell, he still can, right?

"C'mon, Mike," Cam says, jostling him with his elbow. "We're gonna hang at Meckles', maybe get some music done."

Mike nods. "Yeah. Sounds good."

Deanna drapes herself over Cam's shoulder and says, "So have you written your speech yet, Mike?"

Mike pauses, spoonful of pudding touching his lips. "Um. What?" He crinkles the plastic of his Snack Pack between his fingers.

"Your election speech," Deanna says, grinning like she knows Mike's panicking inside. Because he is.

There is no way Mike is giving a speech, especially not in front of their entire class. "Yeah, no."

"You're running against Fitzsimmons and Smith, dude," Cam says. He's absently tapping his fingers on the countertop. They're still waiting for Jason to show up, and Omar and Meckles are doing something loud with Meckles' drums in the basement. Cam hums a couple different melodies once they really get going. The thump-thump-thumping drifts up the stairs, with Omar's bass following Meckles' lead. What they really need is a rhythm guitar, but Cam goes into rants whenever Mike brings it up.

"Fitzsimmons and Smith always run," Mike says. They always win, too; they've been the ruling party of their class since freshman year. Mike is still not giving a speech.

"Right." Deanna bobs her head. "So you'll need a really kick-ass speech."

"Lisa's giving a speech," Mike says. "I'm pretty sure that's enough." Mike has no idea what he'd say. It's not even the thought of standing up in front of a crowded auditorium that's causing him pain here—although that's also not exactly pleasant—it's basically that he has no clear reason for running besides Lisa making him, and he doubts that'll be a point in their favor. And Mike would stab himself in the junk before playing the bi or gay or even the sexually confused card, because Lisa is full of shit.

By the time Jason shows up, fresh from track practice, Mike has eaten three Snack Packs, half a bag of pretzels, and a cherry-flavored ice pop, which he was tempted to shove down Girl Meckles' throat.

Mike loves Deanna, but Deanna lives to torture all her brother's friends—or aggressively date them, in Cam's case, solely to torture her brother. Mike thinks it's a twin thing.

Deanna is giving him these looks. These looks that imply that Lisa has maybe been talking to Deanna about things she shouldn't be talking about.

When Cam disengages the invisible lock that keeps him and Deanna attached at the hip and follows Jay down to the basement, Mike makes faces at Deanna until she waggles her eyebrows back at him. They've always been weirdly good at silent communication, stemming from their third grade bout of chicken pox that kept just the two of them quarantined and crazy-bored for days.

Finally, Deanna huffs out a breath and says, "Nobody told me, doofus. Well, Lisa might've mentioned something, but it's kind of obvious you want Zack to—"

Mike lunges forward and claps a hand over her mouth. What the hell happened to *silent communication*? He knows his eyes are wild, and his face feels hot. "*Please*, Dee," he says, a harsh, panicked whisper.

Her eyes go wide. She uses her fingers to pry his hand off, then cups it between both of hers, pressing it back against his chest. She says, "Hey," only it's a really stunned and subdued *hey*.

"Sorry," Mike says. He still feels like he's been donkey-kicked in the chest. His friends are, like, fifteen feet away; he doesn't need this.

57

"What are you . . . ? Mike, it's totally cool," Deanna says softly.

"Maybe," Mike says. There's nothing wrong with it, he's just not sure he wants even more people to know about something he doesn't even really know about himself yet.

Deanna rings an arm around his neck and tugs him down for a noogie. "It's *totally* cool," she says. "Don't even sweat it, Tate. And you know I won't say a damn thing to anybody, okay?" She lets him go and holds up her little finger, wiggling it in his face. "Pinky swear."

"All right," Mike says, hooking his finger with hers. Deanna has never broken a sacred oath. So far as he knows, she still hasn't told Cam about the Han Solo incident, and even Mike admits that sort of teasing fodder is fucking *gold*. "Pinky swear."

Student council election speech day is pretty anticlimactic. At least it is for Mike, because if they lose, Mike's free of cheesy high school politico, and if they win, Lisa will be happy and hopefully content with her extracurricular schedule, so he's okay with it going either way.

Jules Fitzsimmons and Jeremy Smith are huge nerds— massive math and science nerds, actually. Smith tutored Mike in geometry freshman year—and Mike has no doubts that they'll both move on to impressive nerdy colleges and even more impressive nerdy professional lives, but here and now, listening to Lisa's speech, Mike's pretty sure she's got all of tomorrow morning's votes locked in.

It's maybe got more to do with the way she looks like an otherworldly mermaid in her button-up dress and skin-tight cardigan, long, dark hair spilling over her shoulders, than any of her words, but whatever works. Lisa seriously has bombshell curves. How could he have screwed that up? His hormones are crazy for letting that slip away.

When his name's called, Mike waves, and then he slumps low in his chair to the right of the podium, crossing a leg to rest his ankle on his knee. Principal Lord frowns at him, but Lisa's all they need, anyway. Whatever Mike could say would just ruin their chances. He's better at being silently supportive in the background, like Lieutenant Worf to Lisa's Captain Picard. And Mike is totally blaming Jason for the Trekkie reference—Mike used to be cooler than this.

Fitzsimmons' speech is boring and predictable.

Smith's speech is better, but Mike's afraid that's mainly because of the angle Mike's sitting at and Smith's tight pants. So maybe, Mike thinks grudgingly, he'd had a tiny, inadvisable crush on his math tutor once upon a time . . . Ugh, it's like all his memories are warped now; mutual respect over fractals has now become more about Smith wearing tight pants back before tight pants were even in style.

At the end of the assembly, Lisa collapses into Mike's side and says, "The suspense is going to kill me before tomorrow. You need to buy me pizza."

Mike arches an eyebrow. "Why can't Larson buy you pizza?"

Lisa's nose wrinkles. "He's lactose intolerant." She sounds a little more disgruntled than Mike personally thinks lactose intolerance warrants. As a relationship hurdle, it's not as devastating as, say, being the wrong gender.

"Huh," Mike says. "Trouble?"

"Is it even physically possible to be allergic to plastic?" she says.

Smith says, "You can be allergic to pretty much anything," following them off the side of the stage.

Mike tries to give him a mind-your-own-business glare over his shoulder, but Smith just grins, and Mike remembers why he always enjoyed listening to Smith wax dreamily about dodecahedrons. He fights off an answering smile and shakes his head, deciding to just ignore him.

"All right," Mike says to Lisa. "I'll buy you pizza. Then you can tell me what's up with Larson, and if I'm going to have to get Meckles to kick his ass."

Lisa says, "Nothing's up with Larson," in a tone that suggests nearly everything is up with Larson, but not necessarily in bad ways. "Did you know he's afraid of llamas?"

"Llamas can be scary," Mike says. He's not going to knock a fear of llamas. They've got weird tongues, and Mike's no stranger to irrational fear himself.

"It's his biggest fear, being eaten by a llama," Lisa says. "I don't even think they eat meat."

60

"Llamas eat shrubs and grass and hay," Smith says. He's trailing them like a puppy. Mike is trying hard not to notice.

"Right." Lisa pauses in the hallway and nods at Smith. "So my point," she says slowly. "My *point* is that Larson is weirder than I originally thought. It's kind of neat."

Mike thinks *okay*, eyebrows raised, and stuffs his hands into his jeans pockets. The moment isn't exactly awkward, but he's still wondering why Smith is just hanging around, standing there with them.

Smith smiles down at the linoleum tile. He clears his throat and says, "I, um. Mike, I wanted to ask you . . . You're friends with Mo Howard, right?"

Mike stares at the top of Smith's head, then looks at Lisa. Lisa shrugs.

"Yeah," Mike says, frowning.

"So, uh." Smith rubs a hand under his ear, bites his lip. He darts his gaze up to Mike and then away again. "Never mind."

"Really?"

"Yeah, I—"

"Jeremy," Fitzsimmons says sharply. The click of her heels echoes in the near-empty hallway, and she snaps her fingers. Smith straightens up like a soldier; she's trained him well.

Mike still wants to know what this is about, though. "What do you want with Mo?" he asks, the words coming out a little harsher than he'd meant.

But Fitzsimmons' eyes narrow, and she's drawing up her breath like a fiery dragon getting ready to blow.

Smith swallows hard and says, "Never mind," again, and then he heeds Fitzsimmons' silently beckoning finger and trots off down the hall after her.

"What did he think I was going to do?" Mike asks Lisa, confused.

"Beat him up, probably."

"Beat—" Mike cuts himself off, incredulous. Mike doesn't *beat people up*, first of all, but that's not what he meant.

Lisa cocks her head. "No, you're right," she says. "He was probably worried about Jules beating him up. You, he kind of hero-worships."

"Hero?" No, no, really, he's not going there. He waves a hand around. "I mean about *Mo*," he says.

"The conversation was kind of disjointed," Lisa points out. She grabs his arm and starts pulling him down the corridor, toward the back doors that open up onto the parking lot. "But luckily I'm fluent in Socially Awkward Boy speak."

Mike's sure that's a dig on him, but he doesn't comment.

She grins at him and holds up two fingers. "One of two things," she says. "He was either seeking your permission to ask Mo out—"

"Why?"

"I told you, Mo's been crushing on you for over *two years*, Michael. She has a secret blog dedicated to your loser band."

"She does not," Mike says, but *wow*, if she does, that's kind of awesome.

Lisa flicks the side of his head. *"Or,"* she says, "he was just fishing for Mo-info, since you guys are so friendly-like."

"She's a Bobcat," Mike says. He meant to say that he hardly knows her outside of English and baseball, but it came out wrong.

Lisa has that half-indulgent, half-exasperated look on her face, like she wants to pat his head and say, *And you're* special.

"Shut the fuck up," Mike says gruffly.

Lisa palms the heavy metal doors and pushes out. The afternoon sun is golden already, hanging low, and there's an autumn bite in the wind.

"Pizza," Lisa says, steering him toward her car.

"Pizza, right."

Mike is sixteen and a guy. Mike thinks about sex roughly every other second, which he's pretty sure is normal. So now he's just . . . got more options. It's not that bad, right? Theoretically, it should be awesome.

It's just. He got the girl stuff down in eighth grade, when he'd made out with Carina Constantinides in Cam's basement, and Carina Constantinides had been *thorough*. He mostly knows what he's doing with girls, making out wise. He has no clue what to do with another guy's dick, and so far all he can imagine is unmitigated horror and embarrassment fumbling through trying to figure that out. He's too old for this shit.

"You are not too old, Michael," Lisa says, grabbing another piece of pizza. "God, you're almost seventeen, this is, like, the *best time* to experiment."

"Experiment with what?" Cam says, sliding into the vinyl seat next to Lisa. He waggles his eyebrows.

"Farm animals," Lisa says smoothly. "So we know you're all set."

Cam tugs his newsboy cap to the side, so the brim is just over his right ear. He clasps his hands together and leans into the Formica. "Is this about Meckles' crush on Dotty? Because I know we all decided many, many years ago that Meckles was possibly an amphibious alien, but I think we should all be adults about this."

"Amphibious?" Mike says.

"Hell, yeah," Cam says. "Big words are in, man. I've got ambidextrous on the back burner."

Mike shakes his head. Lisa looks amused, but really it's not even worth laughing over. Cam is totally serious.

Cam steals the half a slice left on Lisa's plate. "So what are you ladies talking about?"

"Have you ever been attracted to a guy?" Lisa asks, and Mike tries to burn her alive with his eyes. Tragically, it doesn't work.

"Dude, Tobey Maguire," Cam says.

Mike stares at him.

"What? Isn't this one of those 'Tobey Maguire is universally hot' things?" Cam says. He stuffs the crust into his mouth and crunches through, "I mean, who doesn't want to fuck Tobey Maguire, right?"

"For the record," Mike says, raising his hand.

Lisa joins him and says, "Yeah, and that's Johnny Depp, anyway, you weirdo."

"What the fuck? Come on, he's Spider-Man. And Johnny Depp is old." Cam makes a face.

Mike can't believe he's actually having this conversation. Wait, scratch that. This is Cam. He grins, shakes his head and says, "Why are you even here?" He's pretty sure Cam had plans with Deanna.

Cam reaches over and snags Mike's chocolate milk shake. "I'm thinking about bringing the fanny pack back," he says.

"Of course you are."

Cam says, "It's ten times cooler than the man purse," like this is a hard feat to accomplish.

"Good luck with that," Lisa says.

Cam gives her a finger gun, because sometimes Cam has trouble acting like a real person. "Luck's got nothing to do with it."

• • •

Smith sits one row away from Mike in homeroom, so Mike can see the blatant relief on his face when the loudspeaker announces Lisa and Mike the winners of the junior class election. Which makes Mike think that his new VP role is going to suck even more than he'd originally suspected.

Cam leans over and claps him on his shoulder. "Congrats, man."

"Yeah, this is great," Mike says, frowning. He probably should've asked Lisa what being on the student council actually entails. Oh god, what if he has to organize *school dances*? What if he actually has to *go* to school dances?

He can't think of anything more horrifying than that.

seven.

Rosie and Mike destroy the living room in favor of making an epic fort. It's a massive, misshapen fortress of cushions, and they use every clean sheet set and blanket they can find. They make sure to cover the TV, too, so they can watch movies.

Their mom comes out once while they're building it, shakes her head, and then disappears back into her office.

They've got a pile of junk food and soda, because it's Sunday morning and Mike doesn't feel like doing anything else. Under the sheet dome, boarded between cushions, he's well aware that he's hiding. He thinks Lisa wants his help brainstorming for Homecoming, and if Mike gets caught up in that crap he's pretty sure his brain will just liquefy right out of his skull.

"Sandwich thinks we should get a bird," Rosie says, stuffing a cookie into her mouth.

"Yeah? What kind of bird?" Mike asks.

"A Tiki Room bird," Rosie says. "That talks."

Mike nods. "A parrot. Good idea. But you better do your

research before asking Mom." Mom's all about being prepared. That's the only reason Rosie has hermit crabs. Mike
coached her for weeks on proper hermit crab care. They'd
even set up the aquarium with an egg to show Mom how
careful Rosie would be with them. The only thing so far that
research hasn't worked on is dogs, but that's mainly because
Mom's allergic. And maybe because Rosie forgot to feed the
practice dog for a couple days, no biggie. It's not like a roll of
toilet paper can actually die.

Rosie looks up at him, mouth pursed. "Birds are easy."

"You think?"

Rosie nods.

Mike says, "So you're sure they don't crap wherever they
want? Mom'll be pissed if a bird ruined the couch because
you figured it'd be polite enough to use the toilet."

Rosie narrows her eyes, thinking. "Maybe he'll scratch
at the door?"

"With his beak?" Mike isn't trying to talk her out of this.
He'd totally be okay with a bird, so long as Rosie knows how
to take care of one. He has a feeling birds are hard, but
Rosie's got a good brain for a six-year-old, so she'll figure
that out.

"Yeah," Rosie says. "Birds are smart."

Mike ruffles her hair. "You can look it up on the computer
later, okay?"

Rosie gives him a cookie from the pile she's hoarded

on her side of the fort. It's one of her favorites, oatmeal chocolate chip, so Mike eats it quickly before Rosie can change her mind.

He plans on eating his weight in cookies and cheese curls and M&M's before he has to get up off his ass and go to work.

Mike works part-time at Louie's House of Cheese. Louie is his mom's younger brother, and he's crazy. Mike's pretty sure that's where Rosie gets it from. He wears a lot of plaid and talks with a French accent. Uncle Louie isn't French. Mike's mom's people hail from Detroit, and out of the long line of Detroit Tates, none of them ever came from France.

He makes delicious spreadable sharp cheddar, though.

Occasionally, Mike works at the House with Chris Leoni. Leoni is Wallace's best friend, and Mike and Leoni have been locked in a battle of mutual hate ever since freshman year, when Mike had taken exception to Leoni taunting Meckles—obviously before Meckles grew to roughly the size of a bear. They glare at each other over the wine and cheese tasting counter, but they have a no-fighting rule while in the store, and they never rat each other out when they sneak sips of whatever bottles of wine Uncle Louie has stashed in the mini-fridge for the day. Neither of them wants to lose their jobs, because working at Louie's House of Cheese is a sweet deal. They get paid to lug cheese around. It's not exactly the toughest thing in the world to do.

Leoni has two inches on Mike, height-wise, and outweighs him by a good thirty pounds, but their mutual dislike usually doesn't get much more physical than Leoni's annoying habit of flicking Mike on the ear.

Mike's having a super fantastic year, of course, so it figures he's not even really paying attention when Leoni takes him down with a flying tackle as he's pulling his jacket on, stepping out of the back of the store. Mike clocks his head on the concrete sidewalk so hard he sees sparks behind his eyes.

"What the fuck, man?" Mike's too stunned to even try to push Leoni off of him.

Leoni grabs the front of Mike's shirt in his fists, leans down close and says—pretty menacingly; Mike's impressed, since Leoni's cursed with a sort of weaselly, high-pitched voice—"You only get one warning, Tate. Be very fucking careful."

Mike's torn between taunting, *Or what?* and asking him what in the actual hell he's talking about. He goes with "Sure, okay," and hopes that gets Leoni off of him. He's heavy; it feels like Mike's hip bones are folding inward and digging up against his spleen.

Leoni releases his shirt and sharply pats his cheek. "Good boy."

Finally, Leoni shifts off of him and gets to his feet. Mike

scrambles up and out of the way and glares sourly, rubbing at his hips. No elbows were thrown, so that's a win, but he hates feeling like he just got bullied. He tugs at the hem of his T-shirt. "You're such an asshole, Leoni," he says, scowling.

Leoni grins at him, stoops to scoop Mike's jean jacket off the ground and holds it out. "Don't forget your coat."

Mike grabs it out of his hands with a huff.

"I need you to get rid of someone for me," Mike says into his cell phone, sprawled on his stomach on his bed. "It's a mercy killing, really. He's too stupid to live."

"I'm not going to kill you," Omar says.

"Ha. Ha."

"How high are you?" Omar asks.

This is a valid question, since Mike hardly ever calls Omar unless he's high. "I'm so stone-cold sober, it's not even funny."

Omar makes a sound of disbelief, but Mike doesn't blame him for his skepticism—it's hard to remember the last time Mike's called Omar without the help of recreational drugs.

"I need you to kill Chris Leoni. Or just make him hurt a lot." Mike would do it himself, except Leoni would probably just sit on him again, which is really uncomfortable.

Omar grunts.

"No, for real! He's a pain in my ass, Omar, and your dad has that whole machete collection in the basement." Omar's

71

dad is badass. He used to take Omar and his two older sisters on wilderness survival trips every year, until Omar got soft and decided he wanted to be a vegetarian. And, okay, Mike knows he's acting a little crazy, but he doesn't actually know what Leoni's beef is. It's just frustrating, and Omar should totally be humoring him here, ugh.

Omar *hmmm*s.

Mike had forgotten how useless Omar is on the phone. He hardly says anything, and Mike can hear faint typing, which means Omar is probably doing homework that Mike should *also* be doing.

Mike asks, "Did you do the worksheet for chemistry?"

"Sure," Omar says. "It's easy. Most of the answers are straight out of chapter five."

Mike sighs. Omar always thinks chemistry is easy, but the good thing about that is he'll help Mike with it in the morning. "And English?"

"Writing my essay," Omar says.

"Right. Instead of doing my bidding or talking me down from my homicidal rage," Mike says. He's cool with either, honestly.

"You don't sound like you're in a homicidal rage," Omar says.

"I'm—huh." Consider Mike talked down. Omar has magical powers, even when he isn't trying. "Thanks. I guess."

"I aim to please."

"Chris Leoni is still a dickface, though," Mike says.

"Amen."

Omar might be a miracle worker, but he's still really unsatisfying to talk to. Plus, now Mike's kind of depressed instead of mad.

"I'm calling Jason."

"You do that." Mike can hear the smile in Omar's voice.

Mike says, "I will," even though he definitely isn't going to call Jason.

Omar says, "Let me know how that turns out for you."

"Fuck you," Mike says without any heat and thumbs off the cell. He drops it on the floor and rolls over onto his back.

He pulls his guitar over and strums the beginning chords to "Confetti," humming absently, but the lyrics make him think about Lisa and J. J. and how dicks have been featured in his last couple jerk-off sessions, and he really doesn't want to dwell on that.

It makes his palms sweat and his head hurt.

He groans and gropes over the edge of his bed for the phone again and calls Jay. He needs a distraction, and Jason's the only one of his friends that he's pretty sure won't be doing anything else.

"Jay, man," he says. "I'm bored, come over and we'll listen to Nick Drake and be emo and shit, you'll love it."

Jason says, "Okay? Should I, um, bring . . . anything?"

Anything is code for weed, and Jason *always* asks this, because Jason still thinks he needs to bribe them all to be seen with him. But after eight months of hanging out,

Jason's actually kind of grown on Mike. He says, "You don't have to bring party favors every time I invite you somewhere."

"But I—"

"Come on, we'll navel gaze and talk about how much we hate our moms."

"I don't—" Jason stops himself, thank god. Sometimes Jason just doesn't get it. Instead, he says, "I think it's shoe gaze."

"You would know," Mike says. "Get your ass over here."

"It's a school night," Jason says, a pathetic last-ditch effort to not come entertain Mike, and what kind of friend is that? Jason apparently knows all his deep, dark secrets now; he has a sacred duty to come over and make sure things aren't weird between them.

"Twenty minutes," Mike says. "I'll make popcorn."

Jason's had the same lame buzz cut for as long as Mike's known him, and it highlights the way his ears stick out like mug handles. And after the month of revelations Mike's just had, he's happy to realize that Jason—and, when he thinks about it, Omar, Meckles, and Cam, also—does nothing for him in the pants department. He supposes they're all objectively handsome. Omar has some sweet arm muscles from playing his bass. Meckles has very large, capable hands; Mike can admit that to himself. Cam has all the appeal of a sack of potatoes, more for the fact that they're practically brothers than any physical lacking. So Mike is saved from the cliché and embarrassment of crushing on his straight friends. Small comfort, but it's something.

Mike leads Jason into the kitchen and hops up onto a stool. "Popcorn," he says, waving the microwave bag in front of Jason's face.

"No, thanks," Jason says, standing in the doorway, hands in his pockets. "Do you have any Diet Coke?"

"Dude." Mike's mind is boggled. Jason needs to consume as many calories as possible just to retain his current human form. "I offer you popcorn, you take popcorn, and you don't ask for diet *anything*. It's like listening to Dishwalla instead of Ash."

Jason has a slight smile on his face. He shrugs a shoulder and says, "Aren't they practically the same thing?"

"I don't think you can be in my band anymore," Mike says, but inside he's secretly proud, because that's exactly something Omar or Meckles would say. Not Cam, though— that's one of the things Mike respects most about him. Despite Cam's lamentable fetish for Jimmy Buffett, Mike and Cam were both musically reared by Zack, cutting their baby teeth on the underrated awesome of Ash and Nada Surf, mortal enemies with the likes of Dishwalla, the scourge of alt rock. Important lessons were learned.

Mike sets the popcorn bag down and goes to the fridge. He pulls out two bottles of Pepsi and tosses one to Jason.

"Come on, let's go to my lair, we can—" He cuts himself off, because lair-haunting usually involves pot, and Mike currently isn't imbibing, and he's got nothing for them to do, otherwise, since Meckles stomped on his PS3 and Mike's mom refuses to replace it.

Crap. They're totally going to end up talking about their feelings.

Upstairs, Jason drops down onto the floor, back against Mike's bed, and Mike turns on the TV, sprawling out on his mattress. He stares at the ceiling and thinks about all the possible things they could talk about that are not the giant elephant sitting in the corner of the room—banjos, Nada Surf, *Manos: The Hands of Fate*, body glitter—and ends up saying, "So. Cam's end-of-the-summer blowout," anyway, before he can stop himself. It's like his brain just doesn't want him to be happy.

There's ominous silence.

Mike feels like there's a lead ball sitting in the bottom of his stomach and he twists his fingers into his sheets to stop them from shaking. Jason hasn't *acted* any different around Mike, but that doesn't have to mean anything.

He takes a deep breath and levers up on his elbows. "Jay?"

Jason's eyes are huge when he turns to look at Mike, and his skin is this pale gray. "I don't know anything."

"Sure you don't," Mike says. He's kind of sickly amused by how uncomfortable Jason is, and he sits up, crossing his legs and leaning his forearms on his thighs. "Lisa says you watched."

Jason's eyes actually get bigger. "No! I mean, uh, watched what?"

Mike snorts. "Come on, Jay," he says, because Jason looks like he's going to throw up, and yeah, this is really kind of fun. "Tell me you didn't want in on that."

Jason goes from gray to flaming red in two point three seconds. He opens and closes his mouth so many times he looks like a fish gasping for air.

"No, really," Mike says, laughing a little, "tell me. Lisa seemed to like all the tongue action."

"I can't—Mike!" Jason flails his arms, banging his elbow into the side of the mattress. Then their eyes catch and he presses a hand over his mouth and starts laughing, too.

Mike flops over onto his side, laughing into his mattress, and his stomach hurts by the time he's trailed off into really kind of unmanly giggles, but whatever. "Jesus Christ," he says, breathless. He leans up onto one arm and peers over at Jason. "I'm fucked up."

"Hey, no." Jason's sprawled out on the floor on his back. He's panting and staring very carefully up at nothing.

Mike says, "Yeah."

Jason rolls his head to the side, dark eyes still sparkling with amusement. It's a good look on him. "You're in no way fucked up," Jason says. "Unless you count everything Cam gets you to do."

This is not exclusive to Mike. Cam's really good at getting people to do shit they would not normally do. "Whatever," Mike says, and then he dials up the volume on the TV.

Mike wakes up five minutes after the time his alarm would've woken him up if he'd bothered to set it before passing out the night before.

Jason is still on his floor. He's got his coat pulled over him like a blanket.

Mike yawns and reaches out to grab a book off his nightstand to peg at Jason's head. It hits him in the shoulder, and Jason just murmurs something unintelligible and rolls over.

Mike spends a few minutes trying to figure out what woke him up, if it wasn't Jason or his alarm, before yawning again and turning onto his other side to find Rosie snuggled up by his pillow.

"Hey," Mike says, his voice an early morning croak.

Rosie says, "Sandwich thinks birds are too much work." She looks disgruntled, like she spent a while arguing with Sandwich about this before grudgingly agreeing that Sandwich was right.

"Sandwich is pretty smart," Mike says.

Rosie harrumphs. "Yeah," she admits.

"Is Mom up?"

"No," Rosie says, and then scoots to the edge of the bed

and hops down onto the floor, presumably to go wake Mom up for breakfast. Rosie's already dressed for school, wearing a too-snug red plaid vest that was part of last year's Halloween costume—she was an insurance salesman—over a T-shirt, olive khaki shorts, and dark purple tights. All the other girls around her age are into sparkles, bright colors, and peace signs. Rosie's T-shirt is the black-and-white Ash one Mike had bought her for her birthday two months ago.

"Was your sister wearing combat boots?" Jason asks sleepily after Rosie clomps out of the room.

Mike sits up, slides his feet off the side of the bed. "She's going through a nineties phase. I blame Pearl Jam. And Meckles." Mike's got nothing against Pearl Jam, honestly, it's just that Vedder's a douche-nozzle. Meckles likes to defend him, because Meckles needs to justify wearing that much flannel in the twenty-first century. Rosie looks up to Mike and his friends, which is only unfortunate when she chooses to emulate Meckles instead of Mike. Still, he approves of the T-shirt and tights.

"Huh," Jason says, and closes his eyes again.

"We have"—Mike checks his phone—"forty minutes to get to school."

Jason says, "Sure," but doesn't move.

Mike chucks a shoe at him.

• • •

"Homecoming," Lisa says, sliding into her seat next to Mike in first period trig.

Mike groans and buries his face in his open textbook. "It's only October," he says, voice muffled. They have Homecoming later than most, because they're the South Morrison Fighting Turkeys, and they always play the Connie Hill Maple Leaves around Thanksgiving. It's tradition.

"Junior Court nominations are in two weeks, Michael."

"And this is important to me why?" Mike doesn't even know what a Junior Court is. The last school function he went to was a sixth grade social. Homecoming is generally a mystery to him.

"Because we need to form a *committee*," she says.

Mike stares at her blankly. Finally, he says, "You want me to be on a committee?" Committees require talking to people who actually care about this shit.

Lisa shakes her head. "I want you to be our class rep on the committee."

"That sounds so much better," Mike says.

"Apparently I have to liaise for the PTO and form inter-class connections or something, so I need *you*"—she tugs a battered manila envelope out of her bag and shoves it at Mike—"to take care of all the preliminary Homecoming stuff. It's the fall prom!"

Mike makes a face, and refrains from pointing out that Lisa never cared about the *fall prom* before. He turns the envelope over in his hands; it's fairly hefty. "What is this?"

"Instructions and guidelines from Mrs. Saunders and Mr. Kerr, our faculty supervisors. Once I figure out what I'm doing with everything else, I swear I'll help you, but for now you're in charge," Lisa says brightly. She's grinning at Mike like she knows this is killing him, and she's so very happy about it. "You need to get three other juniors to join, too."

"You are the worst friend in the history of all friends everywhere in the entire galaxy," Mike says. How the hell is he supposed to get people on a committee about Homecoming? He opens the top flap of the envelope and dumps out the contents—sample flyers, checklists, lots of exclamation points. "This is the shit my nightmares are made of."

Specifically, it's got shades of his current recurring dream where Cam's a sparkly stoner unicorn, Mike's a piece of birthday cake, and everything Meckles says comes out of his mouth as stars and rainbows. There's lots of smiling and laughing and eating of Mike. It's pretty gay, actually. Mike should've seen that coming.

It probably wouldn't take much to get Omar, Meckles, and Jason to join the committee for him, or even Cam, but the problem with making his friends get involved with Homecoming is that they don't really care. Mike doesn't care, either, but Lisa will claw all his insides out through his mouth if he messes this up for her, so what he really needs are a few dedicated yay-school! posers who will do all his work for him.

He has to go to the dark side.

He has to ask the cheerleaders.

The only cheerleader Mike knows personally is Dotty Ramirez, because she's a Bobcat and friends with Mo, and while she's a lousy outfielder and can't catch for shit, she's a good hitter and pretty decent at rounding the bases. Mike has to respect that.

Dotty is almost as tall as Mike, with short, spiky brown hair and a gymnast's build. She has the dubious honor of having been Chris Leoni's first girlfriend, as far as Mike knows, until she stomped on his foot and gave him a bloody nose in the cafeteria last fall.

Mike catches her leaving the field after they beat the lace panties off the Slugs for the seventh time in a row. He says, "I need your help," and Dotty arches an overly plucked eyebrow at him. A bead of sweat runs down the length of her nose and she swipes at it with the hem of her T-shirt, giving Mike an expansive view of her flat, brown stomach and gray sports bra. Mike isn't *unmoved*, but he doesn't bother staring, either.

"Help with what?" she asks.

"Homecoming," Mike says. "Know anyone in our class who'd want to be on a committee?"

"I could ask around," she says, dropping her shirt and placing her hands on her hips. She grins at him, and all her teeth are very, very white. "But only if you can get Meckles to ask me out."

That'll be tough. Meckles is blatantly and irrationally terrified of girls. Mike's got a theory that his compulsive flannel-wearing is specifically engineered to scare off any potential dates.

"How about I get him to at least talk to you?" Mike counters.

Dotty bites her bottom lip. "By Cam's Halloween bash."

"No problem," Mike says. He can loosen Meckles up with beer. It'll be fine.

eight.

An unfamiliar number comes up on Mike's
cell, which is weird, because Mike doesn't get a lot of calls
to begin with. Most of his friends just text him, except for
Lisa and Cam—Lisa, because she doesn't like the detached-
ness of texting, and Cam because he likes to sing into Mike's
voice mail.

Mike warily slides his thumb to answer and says, "Hello?"

"Michael. It's Josh."

No immediate bells are rung. "Who?"

There's a sigh on the other end. "J. J."

"Good Christ, no."

"Yes. Michael—"

"It's Mike. Or Tate," Mike corrects automatically, because
only Lisa, Nana, and his mom call him Michael—and no one
but Rosie calls him Mikey under threat of painful death.

"Michael," J. J. says, and Mike clenches his jaw in irrita-
tion. He hates J. J. so very much.

"What?" he says tightly.

"I was wondering if you'd like to—"

"No."

"—come to a party I'm throwing next weekend. No need to be rude."

"Hell, no," Mike says. He doesn't want to get within ten feet of J. J. He doesn't *think* he'd fall on him sober and try to suck his face off, but he doesn't want to tempt fate.

There's a heavy silence. Then a soft curse and J. J. says, shortly, "Fine," and Mike's surprised to hear some actual hurt in his voice.

Mike suddenly feels a little bad. It's disconcerting. "Uh."

"See you around, Mike," J. J. says, abruptly ending the call. *Shit.* Shit, shit, shit.

Mike presses the edge of his cell into his forehead, eyes squinched up tight. He's such a fucking softy, god, this is J. J. This is the dude who, uh—well, okay, he's never really done anything to Mike, specifically, except stick his tongue down his throat. Mike's willing to take half the blame for that, though, because he's not a complete asshole. But J. J.'s got a fully annoying and grating personality and an almost permanent sneer on his otherwise perfect, handsome face. And yes, Mike did just think that. Goddamn it.

Sighing, he calls Lisa. When she picks up, he says, "Do you think you can get details about a Junior Meat King party?"

"Er, yeah?"

"Fuck. Fine, okay, do that."

"Do I want to know why?"

"No," Mike says. "No, you really don't."

• • •

For the rest of the week, Lisa gives him weird looks while Mike keeps his trap shut, because the last thing he needs is more witnesses for whatever disaster is going to go down on Saturday night. He doesn't even know what he's doing. Does he show up with an apology? Is J. J. going to assume his presence is a come-on? He half thinks he just shouldn't go at all, but there's that little niggling thread of guilt, and Mike just kind of wants the whole thing to be over with. Maybe he'll sit Scalzetti down and explain how very, very drunk he was, and how it'd all been a harmless little mistake.

On Friday, Cam grins across the table at him at lunch and says, "Word on the street is we're crashing Scalzetti's this weekend."

Mike glares at Lisa and says, "It's not crashing if you're invited," and he feels only marginally smug at Lisa's fleeting look of surprise before Cam says, "We're invited? That's totally weird."

Even though Scalzetti and the rest of the Our Lady crowd frequently show up at Cam's parties—Cam's got an email chain set up—they've never before returned the favor.

"Kind of," Mike acknowledges. He doesn't really want to specify that *he* was invited, not all of them together, because Cam's not dumb, no matter how stupid he acts. He'd know something was up.

Omar palms his apple, pushing his tray farther onto the table with his elbows. He says, "Scalzetti likes Mike."

Mike almost has a heart attack before realizing Omar meant that in the totally platonic way. Probably. He barely manages to choke out, "He does not!" anyway.

Omar eyes him oddly. "Chill, man. I spent an hour with him at Cam's last party, talking about the band. He likes the way you play."

"He totally wants to be your groupie," Cam says, doing something obscene with his tongue, because Cam's a dirty pirate hooker.

Jason snorts a laugh into his soda can and Mike kicks him in the shin.

Things are getting out of control.

"It's just a party," Mike says with a tight shrug. "Not a big deal."

Lisa's face says maybe he's *making* it a big deal. He swallows hard and takes a bite of his sandwich and very carefully avoids everyone's eyes.

Cam spends the rest of lunch talking about hats and the merits of facial hair—"I'm thinking about going for the Abe Lincoln," he says. "You know, party around the jaw, business above the mouth."

Mike's totally okay. He's not going to freak out, now that they're all going to J. J.'s party. In fact, it'll end up being better, because it's not like J. J. can expect him to do anything in front of his friends. Mike just has to stay sober and clear-headed.

Piece of cake.

The Scalzettis, Mike knows, live in the gated community of Richmond Plains. Mike's pretty sure their McMansion has a live-in maid and a cook. J. J.'s party isn't at the Scalzetti house, though. Lisa's intel says it's at an old farm property ten miles out of town, and they barely need directions—you can hear the music and see the bright spotlights from about a half mile away.

There's a massive crowd of bikers—leather, tats and all—hanging around fire-lit oil drums when they pull in, and Cam says, "Holy shit," his voice filled with awe.

At least twenty cars and just as many motorcycles are squeezed into a small plot of dirt next to a dilapidated farmhouse, which is covered in overgrown weeds. There's one big bonfire surrounded by half-log benches. A green-and-yellow tractor is pulling a hay-filled wagon around an empty, fenced-in pasture, and a goddamn horse is chomping away at a patch of tall grass, big head hanging out of the Dutch door of an adjoining barn.

Mike thinks it's got to be an elaborate joke.

It's not at all what he had been expecting.

"Is that a *biker gang*?" Cam asks, incredulous.

Mike wants to say no, because that's just ridiculous, right? But he's pretty sure they *are*. Why the hell would J. J. have a motorcycle gang at his party? The crowd's a mix of adults, teenagers, and kids, and even though there's a ton of people there, Mike kind of has the feeling that this is more for family than casual school friends. It makes Mike feel even weirder about being there.

Cam drags Omar and Deanna off to stare in wonder at the bikers. Mike just hopes nobody gets killed. Cam isn't exactly subtle about anything.

Mike spots J. J. down by the hayride, back to the fence, face tilted down to talk to a kid who looks about twelve, her head coming up to his shoulder. He's got jeans on. Not just jeans, but *worn-in* jeans. J. J. tucks one hand in a pocket, the other dragging up his nape to ruffle his hair.

J. J. has a thin neck. And thin wrists, pale, like they haven't seen the sun for a while, if ever, and he's got the shoulder width of a baby bird. He's probably got delicate collarbones, and, like, a concave chest or some shit. Mike should really not ever picture J. J. shirtless, fuck, he's putting too much thought into this.

"Are you seeing this?" Mike hisses in Lisa's ear. "How could I have hooked up with that? He's like an ostrich with pretty hair."

"I don't know, he's got nice legs," Lisa says thoughtfully.

"Not helping." Neither is the fact that J. J.'s smiling at him now, and that his face is actually as handsome as Mike remembers it being. Mike's cheeks heat, because nothing says giant girl like a good, old-fashioned blush.

J. J. slowly makes his way over to them, and there's a lazy hitch to his step that makes Mike think he's more comfortable here than he is anywhere else. "Michael," he says, "glad you could make it."

Jason snickers—he's getting too big for his britches. Mike approves of a little attitude, but Jason better watch out. Mike gives him the evil eye, but Jason just smiles wider, like he thinks he has Mike's number. He probably does.

J. J.'s grin falters when Mike doesn't say anything back, and Mike quickly says, "Yeah," gruff, just because he doesn't want to be rude.

Jason coughs a laugh into his fist.

Seriously, he hates everybody.

Bobbing his head a little, J. J. says, "Right, so. There are sodas and beers and grills over on the other end of the clearing. Please make yourselves at home." He looks up at Mike through his eyelashes and something in Mike's chest gets tight.

Weird.

It's twilight, but almost everything is bathed in gold from the various fires scattered around. He's kind of mesmerized by the way shadows cut sharp lines along J. J.'s cheekbones.

Lisa clears her throat and says, "Jay and I are just gonna go, um, get something to eat."

Mike could man up here and figure out what the hell is going on with his hormones, or he could take the coward's way out and latch onto Lisa. Mike wants to be the good guy, he really does, but strange attraction to J. J. aside, he really doesn't like him.

He says, "Hold up, I'll come with," and pretends not to see J. J.'s disappointed frown.

Mike is not drunk later when J. J. catches his arm and tugs him into the dim shadow of a gigantic oak tree, just outside the firelight cast by the main bonfire. Mike definitely isn't drunk when J. J. leans his full weight all along Mike's front. He's just about three inches shorter than him, and Mike has to tip his head down to look him in the eyes. They're dark, and a little unfocused, and he smells like wood smoke and beer.

Mike grimaces, placing palms on J. J.'s waist and leveraging him away. "This isn't a good idea."

"Why not?" J. J. says, smirking at him.

"Because this isn't a thing," Mike says. "Between us, I mean."

J. J.'s smirk turns sly, which is good, because it gets Mike pissed, which is how he *should* be around J. J.

"Right," J. J. says.

"Look." Mike pauses, because he'd rather carve out his eyeball with a spoon than have this conversation with J. J., but something has to be said. "Look," he starts again, "there's some stuff I have to work out on my own."

J. J.'s eyes narrow. "Okay."

"And you really fucking annoy me, most of the time," Mike says. By breathing, or cocking his hip, or smirking in his face, or . . .

God, J. J. is the motherfucking enemy! This was a bad idea, coming here.

J. J.'s eyes narrow more, and his mouth tightens, and the angles of his face get mean. Mike isn't exactly sure how he does it, but there it is. "All right," J. J. says. He takes a slow step backward, and rubs a hand over his chin.

He looks speculative, and Mike thinks for a split second that J. J.'s gonna go for blackmail, except this isn't a bad teen romance, and if they're both gay here—or bi, or *whatever*—J. J.'s got his own coming-out drama to deal with. They don't need to screw each other over on this. Mike even says that, and J. J. nods.

He says, "You're right, of course, even though I really wish you weren't." He sighs and lightly touches Mike's hair where it falls over his temple. "I don't know what it is about you, Michael. You have entirely too much nose and your eyebrows need a vigorous grooming—"

"Gee, thanks."

"—but I really want to stick my tongue down your throat and suck on your very nice bottom lip."

Mike's mouth dries up. "Uh."

J. J. smiles and walks away, throwing a fruity "Ta" over his shoulder.

Mike's left feeling equal parts horny and disgusted. "I'm too sober for this," he says to himself, slumped back against the rough bark of the tree. What the actual fuck just happened?

But clearly, something about J. J. turns him on. He's willing to admit it was nice, the hard planes of J. J.'s body pressed up along his own. It felt . . . not exactly foreign, but really fucking different anyway. J. J. is sharp all the way around; there's no mistaking him for a girl. With a deep, bracing breath, Mike pushes himself upright and steps out into the firelight again.

Cam calls across to him, "Dude, *s'mores!*"

Chocolate, always good for what ails you. Mike pulls himself together as best he can and goes back to his friends.

Mike isn't sure what he was expecting to get out of the night, but whatever it was, he doesn't feel like he got it. He feels sort of lost, sprawled across the all-the-way-back seat in Omar's van, head pillowed on Lisa's thigh.

He somehow has to deal with the reality that he finds J. J.

hot even without being blind, stinking drunk. So, drunken guy make-out? Probably not an anomaly. If he's honest with himself, the thought of sticking a hand down the back of J. J.'s pants kicks his heartbeat up a lot faster than the hands-on reality of touching Lisa's boobs. It also scares the shit out of him. Almost first-wet-dream scary, with the same mix of shame, embarrassment, and *hell yes.*

It'd be a lot easier if he just liked girls. And he's actually starting to think that he maybe doesn't really like girls at all, or he's leaning so far into the dude side of the Kinsey scale that he *might as well* not like girls at all. Scary, and kind of depressing.

From his position, Mike can just make out Girl Meckles' teased-up Mohawk, a couple messy strands trailing along the seatback in front of him. Cam has his head tipped back, snoring. He can hear Omar and Jason talking in low voices up front, but he can't make out their words.

Lisa smooths hair off his forehead, humming absently.

Mike says, "Hey," softly.

When Lisa looks down at him, he can't quite parse her expression. Too many shadows fall over her eyes and mouth. Her hand slides down to his collarbone and she says, "Yeah?"

"Why didn't you bring Larson?" he asks. He can feel Lisa's leg tense under his head.

"I thought you didn't like him," she says, almost tentatively, which sits strangely on her. Lisa isn't really tentative about anything, she's always the first out of the gate, damn the man, straight on till morning.

And Mike doesn't know why that would matter, anyhow. So he thinks Larson's not good enough for her, so what? He doesn't think Cam's good enough for Deanna, but that doesn't stop them. He reaches up and tugs on an end of Lisa's long, dark hair.

"Bring him," he says. "Next time."

Shadows still hide her face, but her fingers are light, tapping at the side of his throat, and he can almost, *almost* see her smile.

nine.

At the first official Homecoming commit-tee meeting, Dotty brings her cheer-pal Lenny Lad. Mike hasn't had face-to-face contact with Lenny since the fourth grade, when they'd both had a brief imaginative stint pretending to be Russian spies. Mike doesn't hate her or anything; she's just in all the smart classes, so it's not like they've had any reason to talk.

She's kind of a flirt, though, and Mike has to move out of the way when she sits down and flutters her eyelashes at him. Mike leans around her and says to Dotty, "I needed three of you."

Dotty rolls her eyes. "Relax, he's on his way."

He turns out to be Rook Wallace. Of course. Mike didn't honestly expect anything else, given the way his cookies have been crumbling.

Wallace slides into the room just this side of breathless, black curls a mess, like he's run sweaty hands through it over and over again.

Mike says, "Don't you have basketball practice?" Their season just started. No way would the coach let him skip.

"I'll make it if we hurry this up," Wallace says, dropping into the empty seat next to Mike. He grins with his eyes, looking straight at Mike, like he's daring him to say something about being late.

Mike settles back down in his chair with a scowl.

The committee is meeting twice before Royal and Junior Court nominations, and then twice a week after that to organize the theme, refreshments, and decorations, and any other major and minor things that come up before the big day.

Besides the four of them, there are five seniors that Mike recognizes but has never interacted with before, including the senior class vice president. Right now they're arguing, as far as Mike can tell, about the validity of self-nominations. They've been here before, obviously, and Mike just lets them hash it out without him. He broods to himself, scribbling a dark patch of ink on his notebook and thinking up ways he can make Lisa pay. There aren't many he can actually pull off.

Homecoming is not really as big a deal as TV and movies would have him believe. At least, Mike doesn't think so. Their football team is mediocre, even though their marching band is *amazing*, and no one Mike knows personally has ever even been to a post-game celebration. Unless he counts getting plastered with the drum section last year, but, look, Mike has weaknesses, and one of those weaknesses is the sharp precision of fifteen snare drums doing their thing.

Of course, Mike's never been an upperclassman before.

Wallace jostles his elbow and Mike startles out of his daze and glares.

"What?" Mike says.

Wallace ducks his head down close to his ear, and Mike refuses to flinch away when warm, damp breath ghosts over his cheek. "I hear the Bobcats are the undefeated champs of intramural baseball," he says.

"We still have one game left," Mike says, but he can't stop the slight flush of pride. The Bobcats are annihilating the Slugs, and it doesn't hurt that Wallace called them Bobcats instead of the Blue team, which Higgins still insists on using, because he's a tiny, stubborn douche bag.

"You and Scott should think about trying out in the spring," Wallace says.

"Uh, yeah, no," Mike says, because he doesn't think he can be on the same field as Wallace without trying to take his head off with a baseball.

"I mean it," Wallace says in this really earnest voice. "We could use you."

Mike doesn't bother pointing out all the crap that went down before, in their Little League, because if Wallace is going to pretend it never happened, then Mike can do that, too. It doesn't mean he can forget about it, though. Those weren't exactly the happiest times of Mike's life, despite his love of playing the game.

"Forget it, Wallace," Mike says shortly.

Wallace's forehead wrinkles, like he can't figure out what he said wrong, and Mike ignores him for the rest of the hour.

Cam shows up for their final baseball game against the Slugs wearing a fanny pack, BluBlocker shades and a mustache. He's got a red-and-orange Hawaiian shirt open over his Bobcats tee, and his hair is being held off his forehead by a stark white visor, *Hang Loose* etched in neon green puffy paint around the band.

"Hang loose?" Mike says.

Cam grins and says, "I needed a catchphrase."

"That's the catchphrase of the entire state of Hawaii," Omar points out.

"Aloha." Cam waggles his thumb and pinky in the air, like he's a surfer dude instead of a denizen of a town where the largest body of water is the drainage ditch behind the SuperFresh. "Now," he claps his hands together gleefully, "are we ready to take these dudes down?"

"Hell, yeah," Mike says.

"What's with the facial hair?" Omar says, still staring at Cam. "Is that real?" He pokes at Cam's face curiously and Cam slaps away his finger.

"No touching the lip wig," Cam says.

Omar mouths *Lip wig?* at Mike, but Mike has no clue. It's not worth it, trying to figure Cam out—part of Cam's special brand of charm is the screwed-up mystery meat that masquerades as his brain. Besides, they're wasting valuable daylight.

The afternoon is overcast, and since it's the end of October, it's getting pretty dark early anyway. There are no lights over the community center diamond, so by the time they're starting their ninth inning, Mike can barely see the ball. He's in the outfield when Weedy Jim swings blindly and gets off a lucky hit, a homer that sails over Mike's head. Then the heavens open up.

It pours, sheets of cold, heavy rain, and Mike has trouble seeing past the end of his nose, hair hanging lank in his eyes.

It doesn't matter, though. Even with the home run sending two other runners to home plate, the Bobcats are still ahead by four. Higgins ends up calling the game, disgruntled and looking like a drowned rat, and that's it. The Bobcats are undefeated, and Mo leaps at Mike with a loud whoop.

He almost drops her, but instead she wraps her legs around his waist, tilts her head back and yells up into the rain.

She's kind of awesome. It sucks that Mike feels next to nothing for her.

He slides her back down to her feet just in time for them both to be tackled by the rest of their team, and Mike goes down face-first into the mud, laughing.

• • •

Going out for pizza is the time-honored, postgame tradition of winning baseball teams everywhere, but they let the Slugs tag along, too. They're soaked to the bone, muddy and triumphant—or muddy and halfway resentful—and they fill up at least half the restaurant, rowdy enough to get glared at by the waitresses but not enough to get kicked out the door, despite tracking dirt everywhere.

Mike gets shoved into a booth next to Omar. He's twisted so his back is pressed against the wall so they can pack three on the bench, which is next to impossible, even if one of them is tiny and Mo.

"Nice hit," Mike says across the table to Weedy Jim, who is comically squished between Dotty and Cam. Cam's got an arm around Jim's shoulders, and the kid's got a nervous-mouse expression on his face, hands clasped together and knuckles white.

"Thanks," Jim says tightly.

Cam calls him his "little buddy," and settles his visor on Jim's head—apparently Cam lost his lip wig somewhere out on the field, thank god. Jim seems torn between pleased and *oh god, he's going to eat me*; Cam sometimes has that effect on people.

Mike eats five slices of pizza and feels like he's going to throw up, but it's still a good kind of full. He actually feels normal for once, like he's not overanalyzing every scrap of thought in his brain, the way his thigh is pressed warm next to Omar's, the way Dotty keeps kicking at his feet, the way Cam laughs with his head tipped toward Jim.

His shoulders are loose and there's a swing in his step when they leave the restaurant, so it figures that Omar falls in next to him on the way over to his van and says, "So what's going on with you?"

Mike shrugs. It sucks that Omar's always so perceptive. Omar's also probably the least judgmental of all of them, but when Mike opens his mouth all that comes out is, "Nothing."

Omar arches his eyebrow, because Mike always tries that shit with Omar, and it never ever works. This time, though, Mike doesn't actually want to talk about it.

Omar's still looking at him, though, so Mike says, "Okay, not *nothing*, but I'm good with keeping it to myself right now." He actually is. He's even content, at that exact moment, to have some sort of homosexual earworm vibrating its way through his cochlea toward his brain, where it'll probably set up house and pick out curtains and fuck men. Why not?

It's still drizzling, and Mike flips wet hair off his forehead before grinning at Omar.

Omar nods, a single, slow dip, eyes focused on Mike's face. His mouth pulls up on one side into a smile, and he says, "All right, fine."

• • •

It's kind of a letdown, going to school the next day and realizing that intramural baseball is over. Mike passes a few Bobcats in the hall, people he normally wouldn't have associated with, and feels a weird kind of *Breakfast Club* solidarity with them. It'll fade, there's no way Parth, deputy editor of the school newspaper and a complete control freak, will continue to fist bump him indefinitely, and he's probably only got a week left of exchanging bobcat growls.

Melancholia follows him all through classes and into the next Homecoming committee meeting, and Dotty takes one look at his face and gives him an understanding hug. And then she punches him on the shoulder and says, "Buck up, camper, we won." Dotty has a seriously mean right hook.

"Hell, yeah, we won," Mike says. "We're the Bobcats!" He very carefully doesn't rub the soreness out of his arm, because that's just sad.

Lenny makes a growly sound and giggles, and Mike glares at her a little, because Lenny isn't a Bobcat, but that just makes Lenny roll her eyes.

Mike gets no respect.

"Good for you," Wallace says, and Mike really, really wants that to be sarcastic, but it's not. Wallace is lounging back in his chair, head tipped back to smile up at him. It's not even a practiced, look-at-me sprawl, it's an I'm-really-fucking-exhausted sprawl, pale-faced with faint smudges under his eyes, and yet he still manages to look genuinely happy for Mike.

Wallace, Mike thinks, takes up a lot of space. He's not huge, like Meckles, but he's got a weird fucking presence for an eleventh grader. He's got motherfucking *confidence*; it's enough to make Mike want to punch him in the mouth, mess him up a little. It's just not normal. Mike's itching in his own skin—how can Wallace be so different?

Mike says, "Thanks," because he can totally be polite.

Wallace's grin gets brighter and he pushes out the chair next to him with his foot. "Come on, sit, let's get this meeting rolling." Then he yawns and says, "Fuck, I'm ready for bed."

Mike eyes him warily as he sits down.

Something in his stomach is unsettled, but he can't tell what or why. Then he remembers with a jolt that Wallace has some really damning dirt on him. Involving J. J.

Mike tenses, jerking his head down to stare very hard at the table in front of him.

Wallace nudges his arm and says, "Hey, you all right?"

Mike swallows hard and says, "Yeah." He's definitely not *all right*; he's basically waiting for Wallace to *humiliate* him, but whatever.

And then one of the seniors strolls in with a huge whiteboard and Mike actually pays attention for once, just so he doesn't have to think about anything else.

Friday morning, Mike isn't surprised when Wallace gets a Junior Court nomination. He isn't surprised when Lenny,

Dotty, and Leoni get nominated, too, or even Judge, because he's the closest the school has to a football star, or Carina Constantinides, because she's got huge boobs.

He *is* surprised when they call Mo's name, because Mo has two lip rings and a tattoo of a mermaid on her left forearm and, despite being good friends with Dotty, she doesn't really hang around the kind of kids who think Homecoming is worth anything at all.

He's also really shocked to hear his own name said over the loudspeaker in homeroom.

"What the hell?" Mike says. He's staring up at the speaker attached to the wall above the door, like maybe his brain went crazy and he just heard that wrong. At the meetings, they'd decided that a nom's only accepted if it's been seconded and thirded, so there are at least three people out there who want to torture Mike with a corsage and a suit. When Mike finds out who they are he's going to kick them in the groin.

"Huh," Cam says. He looks genuinely bewildered and surprised when Mike looks over at him, so his balls are currently safe. From Mike, at least.

This is, Mike thinks, the worst thing that could have ever happened. It's bad enough that he has to be on a planning committee for it, and that Lisa probably would've bullied him into attending the actual dance, but now, if he remembers correctly, he'll have to have a *date*, and he'll have to be *presented at the pep rally*, and if there was any way he could get out of this without having Lisa attack him like a jackal, he would.

Seriously, he's such a total pushover. He'd blame Lisa, except it's very obvious that he's always been this way. Lisa's not even the first one to use this power over him for evil; Mike's broken all his limbs at least once because of Cam and Cam's pout and his manic desire to throw himself off roofs and bike ramps and trees. Thank god he has Deanna now, and Deanna's willpower, and if Cam doesn't always listen to her, at least he no longer drags Mike down with him. Most of the time.

"Sucks to be you, man," Cam says.

Yes, it certainly does.

ten.

Cam's end-of-the-summer blowouts are trumped only by Cam's Halloween blowouts. The sucky thing is that costumes aren't requested, but required. For a while there, when they were thirteen and fourteen, it wasn't cool to dress up. Mike loves and misses those times.

There's nothing that Mike hates more than picking out a Halloween costume, but he's basically the only one. Cam, Deanna, and Meckles are filled with little-kid glee, and even Omar's getting into the spirit of the holiday.

Now, Dotty, Lenny, and Mo are happily spending their fourth period study hall in the library making a list of everything that Mike can put together without actually buying anything—that had been his stipulation. He wouldn't be caught dead in Halloween Adventure.

Dotty looks at him thoughtfully. "You know, we're about the same size."

Mike doesn't like where this is going.

First of all, it's pretty crappy when a girl cheerleader in perfect athletic shape says you're the *same size*. Mike might be batting for the other team, but that doesn't mean he is, or wants to be, a girl.

Second of all—Dotty is a *girl cheerleader.*

"You seriously want me to go in drag?" Mike says, most parts of him horrified and just a tiny, quiet part of him intrigued.

"Well," Dotty says, "no."

Mo says, "You'd look pretty hot in a skirt," not helping matters at all. Her eyes say she's enjoying every minute of this.

"It isn't necessarily drag," Dotty says, tapping her forefinger to her bottom lip. "You'd be a guy in my cheer outfit."

Mike doesn't exactly see what the difference is. He'd be a guy in a skirt. Which is good for a laugh, maybe, if you weren't overly sensitive about your sexuality. Mike's totally touchy about that right now.

Lenny snaps her gum. She says, "I like it. No boobs, though."

"Totally not," Dotty says, nodding. "And I'm not giving him my spankies." She makes a face.

Mike isn't sure he wants to know what spankies are, or that he'd want them even if Dotty was offering. He makes a face of his own.

Mo looks like she's on the verge of cracking up. "Oh my god," she says. "Guys, you can't be *serious.*"

Mike points at Mo. "Yeah, see, what she said."

"I'm not saying he shouldn't wear underwear," Dotty says,

and Mo *loses* it, stuffs both her hands over her mouth to help stifle her giggles, because Ms. Horton, the librarian, is glaring unhappily in their direction.

Lenny flips her dark hair over a shoulder and says, completely straight-faced, "He'll have to shave his legs."

Mo practically falls out of her chair, half sprawling all over Mike in helpless laughter, and in Mike's somewhat mad scramble to get away from her—it's a knee-jerk reaction, he's not proud of it—he accidentally kicks the table they're sitting at, tipping it over. Lenny and Dotty yelp, their books and papers go everywhere.

They all end up getting detention, and Mike has a horrible feeling he's just lost a battle that'll cost him the war.

"Why do you hate fun?" Cam says. It's more of a whine than a question.

They're in Meckles' basement, trying to decide what they're going to play the next night at Cam's party.

"I don't," Mike says, not bothering to look up from his guitar. "I hate you."

Cam can badger him all he wants, but there's no way Mike's telling him about his costume. He's still got a half-hearted notion that he can somehow stop Dotty and Lenny from storming his house tomorrow with razors and tweezers and *cheerleading outfits*.

"I told *you* what I'm going to be," Cam says.

"You told everyone," Omar says, and Cam pouts even more.

Cam's going to be Magnum, P.I. The lip wig from intramural baseball had been a trial run.

Mike has weird friends.

"We need a set list," Meckles says.

"Just pick a bunch of Halloween songs. Jay can noodle a *Blade Runner* electronica solo," Cam says, lounging back on the couch. "'Thriller,' *Scooby-Doo*, some Voltaire, Tim Burton miscellanea, 'King Tut,' 'The Monster Mash.'" He hooks his ankle around the mic stand and tips it over to land between his spread legs. He flicks the microphone on and says in his best mad scientist voice, "I was working in the lab, late one night—"

Meckles groans and covers his face, but Jason feeds the beast and starts playing along.

Cam says, "I need background voices, you pussies! Who wants to be Dracula?"

They're the same songs they play every year, but you really can't beat the Halloween classics. Mike joins Omar and Jason on the vocals and tries not to think about how there's a solid chance he'll be flashing the crowd tomorrow under his cheerleading skirt. It's a good thing he has such a nice ass.

Mike can't figure out what Rosie's supposed to be. She's got a gauzy purple skirt on over a pair of jeans, and her face is painted like a cat's. She has spangle bracelets up to her elbows and a blue-and-red Phillies cap on backward. When Mike asks her what she is, Rosie just says, "I'm dressed up."

Mike wishes he could get away with that.

Mom has a tall witch's hat pulled down to her ears, her wild, honey-brown curls eating up the brim. She cackles at Rosie and chases her around the kitchen table, and it's times like these that remind Mike that his mom's pretty amazing.

Mike'll be long gone by the time they get back from the pumpkin festival at the community center, and he's waiting until the very last minute to get dressed. There's no way he's letting his mom see his costume before she leaves.

Dotty and Lenny are doing something scary in his room. He's not ready to face them yet.

When Rosie runs off to find her plastic pumpkin bucket, Mom leans a hip against the kitchen counter, sips at her hot chocolate, and says, "So, Michael. Anything you want to tell me?"

Mike blinks. His mom isn't exactly the heart-to-heart type. She's always been big on letting him learn by screwing up, and he mostly cleans his own messes. Not that she isn't supportive, but she sets out guidelines, not rules, and she tries to make sure Mike's as informed as possible. No set curfew, no parental controls on the cable box or their computers. So thanks, Mom, for all the exploratory gay porn.

"Mike?" she says. She taps the tip of his nose with a finger.

Mike clears his throat and says, "No?"

111

Mom takes another sip of cocoa, watching him coolly. "You know, just because I can be a lax parent doesn't mean I don't check up on you."

"Oh god," Mike says. Hot fear licks up his spine. He deleted his browser history, but Mom has freaky computer skills for an old lady. He never thought she'd use her powers for evil.

"Junior Class Vice President?" She grins, tucks a lock of hair behind her ear. "I'm proud of you. Confused," she concedes, "but proud."

"Um." Mike feels so light-headed and flushed, he might pass out from the sudden rush of relief. "It's Lisa's fault."

"I'm sure," she says. "Lisa's a nice girl."

Mike wouldn't exactly call her nice, but whatever. He nods. His neck feels a little wobbly and his breathing still isn't quite right.

She sets her mug down and says, way too nonchalantly, "Of course, I'm sure you can find lots of nice boys, too."

Crap. The second spike of adrenaline might kill him, he isn't sure.

There's a sly twist to her mouth that has no business being on any mom's face.

Mike says, "Mom, it's not," and stops. He truly has no idea what to say to her. His back is so tight his muscles are throbbing, and he crosses his arms over his chest, tucks his chin down to stare so hard at the counter he has to blink rapidly to keep his eyes from watering. "I mean. Yeah."

She reaches out and squeezes his shoulder, then presses a kiss to his forehead. And then Rosie skips in, swinging her bucket back and forth.

"Ready?" Mom asks.

Rosie gives her a thumbs-up. She'd added about ten multicolored beaded necklaces to her ensemble while she was on her bucket hunt. There's a purple pony sticker on the apple of her cheek.

Mom ruffles Mike's hair and says, "Be good tonight," before ushering Rosie out of the kitchen and toward the front door. Rosie is singing "trick-or-treat" off-key at the top of her lungs.

Mike's frozen in the middle of the room. His skin feels too tight, there's a cold sweat covering his whole body. His mom knows he likes dick. His mom probably found out that he likes dick by watching some choice videos that pretty much scarred Mike for life. He kind of wants to hide in his room for the rest of forever.

On the bright side, though, he just sort of came out to his mom and it went pretty fucking great.

Dotty is a pirate.

Dotty is a fantastic pirate, and in the spirit of fair play, Mike guesses, Dotty is a male pirate, complete with a mustache and beard.

It's not exactly an eye-for-an-eye thing, considering Mike

actually has to shave his legs—all the way up. They let him do most of it himself, locked in the bathroom. He only nicks himself twice, around his knees, but they insist on helping him with the back of his thighs. It's something Mike never wants to experience again.

"Perfect," Lenny says. Mike's pretty sure she's supposed to be a hooker, but he doesn't say anything, because sometimes girls can be sensitive about things like that. Then she holds up Dotty's uniform—white, gold, and maroon and way shorter than Mike remembers.

Mike says, "No."

"Don't be a baby," Dotty says. "This'll be awesome."

"This'll be a *disaster*. I can't even wear my boxers with that, do you know what that means?"

"You're wearing it," Dotty says, in a tone that isn't taking no for an answer. When did Dotty get so fucking *scary*? "So you better find some underwear that'll work." She cocks her head, eyeing his crotch. "Otherwise, it'll just about cover you."

Mike is stunned. Did Dotty really just imply that he go commando in a skirt?

Lenny giggles.

Mike says, *"Fine,"* snatches the uniform out of Lenny's hands and then pushes them out into the hall. He doesn't need witnesses for this.

He digs through his drawer full of boxers until he finds an unopened packet of briefs from Christmas two years ago.

114

They're too small, the band cuts way down low across his pubic bone and his junk is uncomfortable no matter how he positions it, but they'll have to work. He feels ridiculous.

Zippered, the skirt sits high on his waist, the pleats barely falling to mid-thigh, and the sleeveless top stops just above his belly button. He doesn't even bother looking in the mirror. He shoves his feet into his sneakers and opens the bedroom door.

Lenny and Dotty just look at him, silent.

Mike pushes his hair back off his face and glares at them.

"Hi," Lenny says. She sounds a little dazed.

"Wow," Dotty says. "Not entirely hideous."

Mike fights the urge to cross his arms over his chest. "I look like a girl." Thank Christ they didn't make him comb his hair or put on makeup or anything.

"*Definitely* don't look like a girl," Dotty says.

"I think I have a kink now," Lenny says.

Her fingers creep out and Mike slaps them away from the edge of his skirt.

"No, for real," Lenny says, "what kind of underwear do you have on under there?"

"None of your damn business," Mike says, still disgruntled. "Can we just *go*?" The briefs are already working their way into the crack of his ass.

Lenny tugs on her elbow-length, lace fingerless gloves—Madonna? Maybe?—and smooths her hair and does some kind of shimmy with her skirt. Then she says, "Okay, I'm ready."

Dotty says, "Yarrrrrr," and brandishes her plastic cutlass.

Mike huffs and stomps off down the stairs. The skirt flounces up in the back with every step.

Cam's hair is slicked back. He's got on skin-tight bright red jeans, a blue graphic tee with the sleeves rolled up, and wraparound shades. The sunglasses slide down to the tip of his nose and he whistles through his teeth when he spots Mike. He says, "So, you gonna let the quarterback feel you up in the backseat of his Chevy after the big game, or are you gonna make him work for it?"

"Fuck you. Who are you supposed to be?" Mike asks.

"Stiles, Mike," Cam says, smoothing his hands down his chest. It says *Obnoxious: the Movie*—how appropriate. "Check out Dee, she's a total Boof."

Mike checks out Deanna, setting up a snack table across the room. Since Deanna is wearing a black cat suit, Mike figures Cam's trying to sell the *Teen Wolf* movie reference as slang. Mike's going to try his best to ignore that.

"What happened to Tom Selleck?" Stiles from *Teen Wolf* is a pretty obscure costume, even for Cam, who spent two Halloweens trying to convince everyone that a fake beard and a pipe made him Rutherford B. Hayes.

"Dad wouldn't let me get a Ferrari. I wanted to be authentic."

"You should be on medication," Mike says.

"Hey," Cam says, "you're the one wearing a skirt."

Score one for Cam. Mike is indeed wearing a skirt, thanks for the reminder. It's a little drafty, too, considering the time of year. "I was kidnapped by a pirate and a hooker," Mike says.

"A likely story." Cam shoves a plastic cup in his hands. "Go forth, drink beer, avoid Zack, 'cause he'll laugh his ass off at you." He points toward the deck. "Ten o'clock, front and center."

Mike gives him a single finger salute and goes off to grab a beer for the first time in weeks. He's pretty sure he'll need it.

It's not that Cam's dad just lets them have these wild, drunken parties.

It's that Uncle Jem actually thinks Zack is a responsible adult, even though Zack is most definitely *not* a responsible adult. At twenty-six, Zack's got a BS in physical fitness, he lives at home, sells weed to his friends, and works at The Running Place in the mall. When Zack is chaperoning, they usually end up with more alcohol than they know what to do with. He collects everyone's keys at the door, though, before he disappears with his own gang of friends to mingle. No one goes home before dawn.

Mike spots Wallace and Leoni early on—Wallace gives him a little wave across the kitchen; it's totally weird. He takes an awkward swallow of his beer, nodding at him, then thankfully gets distracted by Mo and her pale pink tulle ballerina skirt.

The house is packed by ten and the crowd's spilling out into the backyard. It's so hot inside that the chilly fall weather is a relief. Winter starts early there. It's probably the last time their band'll be able to play out on the deck until the spring.

Cam's deck is not actually attached to the house. It's halfway down the lawn, on the other side of the pool. It's more like a raised platform wired with halogen lampposts and outdoor sockets. Cam's dad had it built because it was either that or let them hold concerts on the balcony off the master bedroom. The deck's for his peace of mind—Cam has a tendency to fall off high things. Or jump.

Someone wolf-whistles when Mike bends over to switch on his amp. He wiggles his ass a little, because he's done being embarrassed. He may not be able to fully own his sexuality, but he can totally own the fact that he's rocking this cheer uniform. The briefs still suck, but the air flow feels great now, and even Lisa had a hard time looking away from his truly spectacular legs earlier. Lisa, who is Hillary Clinton because she's a "woman of caliber." Mike doesn't even think he can blame that on Larson (who came as a *wood sprite*, with fairy wings and everything), because Lisa's been acting like a young primary election candidate ever since the school counselors broke out college applications. Mike thinks she's freaking out about her future.

Meckles is already behind his drum set, warming up. Omar is helping Jason move the Casio, devil and angel on either side of the keyboard. They swear they didn't plan it, but Mike doesn't believe them. Mike plugs in his guitar, plays the opening riff to "Smoke on the Water," and feels awesome about his guitar stance, the way his worn, half-laced high-tops look huge below his bare calves. He's ready to go.

Cam is perched on the railing with Deanna caught between his open legs, making out. Meckles makes a sound like a dying water buffalo and pegs Cam in the back of the head with one of his drumsticks.

"Are we ready?" Meckles says.

Cam peels himself away from Deanna, twists around and hops off the railing and onto the deck. "Hold on to your pants, dude," he says, and Meckles chucks the other stick at him before pulling another pair out of thin air and smashing them onto the high hat. He's fast for a zombie.

Jason doesn't even wait for Cam to grab the mic before rolling into "This Is Halloween."

Mike shakes his head like a dog after setting down his guitar. He's dripping sweat. He hopes this uniform is old, because it's never going to be the same. It's Dotty's own fault for making him wear it. He gets pretty animated on stage, but not nearly as much as he wants to. Sometimes Mike wants to rock out and knock shit over, but if Mike purposefully breaks his amp his mom will never buy him another one, and Meckles would probably stuff his sticks down his throat if he did anything to his precious drums.

Mike's sweat is rapidly cooling in the night air, and by the time he's done wrapping cords and getting his guitar in its case, there are goose bumps popping up all over his exposed skin. He doesn't want to go back inside yet, though.

He leans on the railing next to Meckles, holding a plastic cup full of beer and says, "Dotty Ramirez likes you." He feels like an idiot for saying it, but he'd promised Dotty.

Meckles makes a choking noise. "Um."

Mike knocks his elbow into Meckles' side. "Come on, at least go talk to her."

Meckles had been starting to lose his performance flush, but now the red's flooding right back up his neck to cover his cheeks again. He shakes his head. Mike doesn't know why Meckles is so freaking bashful. He's got that whole Irish brawn going for him, and he's good-looking, even if he's got an overabundance of freckles pretty much everywhere.

Dotty is a Latina goddess. Meckles should be all over that.

Meckles looks at the ground and shrugs.

Mike says, "Do I need to get Girl Meckles over here for a pep talk? Weird twinny mind-melding?"

"No." Meckles looks horrified.

"Well, then. Go talk to Dotty. It'll be fun. I'm not asking you to eat her face or anything." Mike had been aiming for a zombie pun, but it falls kind of flat; he's got a weird, buzzing energy under his skin, like a post-show high but bastardized somehow. It could be the way he's spotted Wallace lurking around, staring at him.

"Go." Mike nudges Meckles again before pushing off the railing and sauntering away.

There's a fire pit down near the woods, and the music's loud enough to carry all the way back to where Mike is standing at the tree line. J. J.'s in front of him, and it's starting to feel like familiar territory.

What Mike realizes about J. J., despite having turned him down, is that J. J. apparently likes to flirt. Specifically, J. J. likes to flirt with *him*, and now that Mike knows he's not going to pin J. J. to a wall and make him pay out what his mouth is so smartly selling—at least, he really hopes he's not—Mike finds he doesn't mind flirting back.

It actually helps that he's wearing a skirt. He's not sure why, but it does. That would probably be shaming if he hadn't let himself relax with a drink or two or three. Or four.

He's not going crazy, but he thinks he deserves a little chemically enhanced relaxation here, especially with Wallace being a creeper.

J. J. makes a fine cowboy, but that might just be the beer talking.

And then Mike compliments J. J.'s boot spurs and J. J. puts a hand on his thigh.

"This is going to a weird place," Mike says. His body isn't completely against it, but his mind is still a shining beacon of opposition. He points off to the left. "Imma walk away now."

J. J. says, "You'd think after so many rejections I'd just give up. There's just something about the way your ass is wearing that skirt."

"Sexual harassment will get you nowhere," Mike says, but he's half laughing, and J. J. trails after him back up to the house.

By three a.m., Mike's relatively sober-headed again. He's around the side of Cam's house, smoking. The party is oddly muffled there, and Mike huddles into himself a little, wishing he'd thought to bring a hoodie. Or pants.

A throat clears, and Mike glances up to see Wallace. Wallace has on a Steelers jersey and jeans, like he half-assed a costume just so Cam would let him through the door.

"What?" Mike says. He'd been expecting something like

this, what with all the weird, sideways glances Wallace has been giving him all night.

Wallace ducks his head, palms the back of his neck, then says, "So. You and J. J."

Ah.

Here. It. Is, Mike thinks. The big moment where Wallace calls him a fag and spits on him. Maybe. Mike's never actually heard him use a slur to someone's face before.

Wallace shifts closer. "Are you—?"

He cuts himself off, and Mike takes a suspicious step back, bringing his heels and the wings of his back as he leans away up against the siding behind him. He stills when Wallace lifts a hand, hovering dangerously close to Mike's cheek, and Mike's frozen for a second, because this is seriously starting to look like some kind of come-on, and there's *no way*—

"Fuck's sake, Wallace, no, I'm not gay," Mike says, defensive, arms crossed protectively over his chest, because he's not coming out to *Rook Wallace*, of all people. No matter what Wallace saw, it's none of his damn business if Mike's bi.

But then he catches sight of Wallace's face. There's a flash of what looks suspiciously like hurt in his eyes before Wallace's lips curl up into a smile that's not really a smile, and something clicks in Mike's brain. Mike's seen that look before. He's seen it on Theo Higgins every time Lisa has to say no. He's seen it on *J. J.*

And Mike is now two for two at alienating people who

apparently like him for some godforsaken reason. He's a total *douche*. He deflates, slumps against the wall. "I mean. Fuck."

There are two main reasons Mike doesn't like Wallace. The first, and most important, is because Wallace used to pound him after Little League baseball games. He's never told anyone that, not even Cam. Mike's pretty sure Wallace hasn't told anybody either, it's kind of their dirty little secret. They'd never been friends, but they'd never been enemies either, and then they both hit twelve and Wallace apparently decided that he didn't like Mike's face. The fact that Wallace used to jump him *alone* made it that much more personal. He hadn't been showing off; he just really, honestly wanted to beat the living shit out of Mike. Mike gave as good as he got, though. They'd both limp home afterward, bruised and bloody, and Mike always gave a tough-game excuse to his mom. And if he cried a couple times alone in his room, well. It was nobody's fucking business.

The second reason is weirder, now that he thinks about it, but no less valid. Two months into high school and it was like someone flipped a switch in Wallace's brain—it's just unnatural, how freaking nice Wallace got. And then the shit-eating grins started, the holding open doors for him, the narrow-eyed stares, the body language that made Mike's entire existence into one big joke. It was like he was no longer significant enough to punch, but ignoring him completely would take too much energy. The biggest insult.

"What the fuck is going on?" Mike says tiredly. "You always—you—don't you *hate* me? What the fuck, you broke my *nose*." It'd bled like a *motherfucker*, too, he'd had to tell his mom he'd accidentally run his bike into a light pole.

"I had some misplaced rage," Wallace says with a casual shrug, like he isn't overhauling Mike's entire worldview, not only turning it upside down but ripping it to itty-bitty shreds. Mike's gonna have a hell of a time trying to piece it back together. "It didn't hurt to have a reason to touch you."

"Uh. Okay." Mike's only option is to suppress this entire conversation. Suppress, suppress, and suppress some more. He has never been more weirded out in his entire life, and that's including the time Mike accidentally caught Cam jerking off to German porn.

Wallace eyes him up and down, head to toe, slow and deliberate. It's enough to make Mike freeze again, eyes saucer-wide. He watches, horrified, as Wallace's gaze catches on his knees, slides up his bare thighs, lingers at the nervous grip Mike has on the hem of the skirt, and gets weirdly hot, the blue iris dark with pupil, on the flesh of his stomach, where the small strip of skin is exposed around his belly button. Mike's suddenly even more conscious of how tight Dotty's top is on him, the broadness of his shoulders making up for the distinct lack of boob.

Wallace's ever-present grin has crept into his eyes now, along with a look of resolve.

Mike has just enough time to think *Wait, what?* before Wallace kisses him.

At first Mike is too stunned to move. He holds himself still for one shocked moment before making an embarrassing sound in the back of his throat and kissing Wallace back.

And, fuck it, it's a *fantastic* kiss. Wallace has firm, dry lips—different from Lisa, from the sticky-sweet lip gloss she always wears—and when Wallace bites his lower lip, Mike instinctively opens up a little, just enough to let Wallace's clever, awesome, *perfect* tongue sneak in and lick over his teeth.

Mike is vaguely aware that he's gripping the front of Wallace's shirt in his fists, like he's trying to reel him in closer. Wallace is standing with his thigh pressed hard between Mike's legs and for a split second, Mike believes skirts are the best invention *ever*, because that's definitely Wallace's hand palming his ass, fingers spread half on the thin cotton of his briefs, half on the bare crease at the top of his leg.

But then Wallace abruptly shifts backward, breaking their mouths apart. His hand slides down to skim the back of his knee—Mike was apparently trying to *climb him*—and gently pushes Mike's leg down so their bodies are no longer touching. He leaves Mike's hands, though, where they've still got a death grip on his shirt.

There's more than a chill in the air, and Mike shivers.

Wallace leans in again, tilts their foreheads together and

breathes; Mike can feel the rapid trip-skip of Wallace's pulse against his thumb.

Wallace says, voice husky, "I'm really sorry you're not gay."

Mike's hands fall limp to Wallace's hips, then fall away completely when Wallace steps back. He says, shaky, "Me, too," but Wallace is already gone.

What Mike doesn't get—besides the fact that Wallace is apparently really fucking self-aware for a seventeen-year-old, and don't think Mike isn't suspicious of *that*—is that Wallace has a hard-on for *him*. Mike. It's kind of surreal. Not exactly frightening, but Mike isn't sure what else to call the weird tingling in all his limbs.

"You all right, man?"

Mike looks over at Omar. His devil horns are crooked, and his eyes are bloodshot. He doesn't look all that sober, which is rare for him. Omar usually likes to keep all his senses in working order.

Mike says, "No, I don't think I am."

eleven.

The Tates' garage is packed with Rosie's old baby equipment, bins of out-of-season clothes, and an over-abundance of kitchen supplies that his mom continually orders off TV, despite being the worst cook in any given universe. It's like she keeps thinking she'll get better if she just has the right tools.

"There is no more normal," Mike says, calling Lisa. His mom's out with the car and he needs to find his bike to get to work.

"Sure there is," Lisa says absently. "Do you think I should let Larson get me a ferret for my birthday?"

"No." Rosie researched ferrets five months ago. They're sneaky, and there's a good chance they'd eat Godzilla and Professor Cheese. Lisa has a house rabbit. "And normal has totally left the building." He hasn't decided whether to tell Lisa about Wallace yet, but he's leaning toward *no fucking way*. Telling someone will just make it a Thing.

A bigger deal than it actually is.

Before, Mike had always liked November. It's a good time of year—not freezing yet, not too rainy. It has Thanksgiving, which, even if it involves crazy Uncle Louie and Nana the Tyrant—he loves his grandmother, but she's retired military and sometimes that's just exhausting—is mostly all about truly excellent food and falling asleep in the living room in the middle of the afternoon, watching football with Gramps.

Now, he's got Homecoming, and Wallace, and he's dreading every second of every day.

It's like the apocalypse came, only instead of nuclear bombs and zombies, Mike gets school participation, gay thoughts, and motherfucking cheerleaders.

He has no idea how to get out of this mess.

Mike had made a list of all the possible reasons Wallace could have had for kissing him, but he didn't come up with a lot. Mike doesn't have many self-esteem issues, but that just means he accepts the fact that he's not perfect. Awesome, yes, a guitar god, obviously, but good-looking? Handsome to the degree that attracts other handsome people? Not really.

Maybe Wallace is just curious. Maybe he's doing some experimenting himself, and Mike seems like a good choice to dick around with.

Safest bet for Mike: stay away from Wallace and keep the status quo. He's got a horrible feeling it's not going to be easy to do.

"I could argue that there was no normal here to begin with, given that Cam is apparently a fully formed, functioning human being. Or I could say that we make our own normal." Lisa pauses. "Either would fit."

"I'm in the running for Homecoming King," Mike says.

"Yeah, that's a little weird."

"You think?" Mike finally finds his bike, but it's under a couple precariously perched boxes. He can't remember the last time he's used it.

Lisa says, "You could run for Queen, but I don't think you're ready for that."

"Why are we even friends?" Mike knocks over what looks like pretty much every kitchen gadget in creation trying to unearth the bike. He kicks boxes aside in a huff; he's going to be late for work.

"Because I let you see my boobs."

"That's a lie," Mike says, walking his bike out into the dying afternoon light. Touch them, yes, but Mike has never ever been allowed to see Lisa's boobs, even when they were dating.

"Oh, that's right, because it would've been a *waste*."

Mike says, "I'm hanging up now, and I'm totally not saying goodbye," and hits End, stuffing the cell into his back pocket. He zips up his hoodie against the cold and sets off down the street.

The House of Cheese is about a twenty-minute bike ride from Mike's house. Not fun, but not hard, either. It's nestled between a consignment shop and a dentist's office, with an ice cream parlor on the corner and a used car dealership on the other side of the street. Since Mike can't really see the appeal of specialty cheese, he has no idea how Uncle Louie manages to stay in business. If they were in a mall, *maybe*, just from curious foot traffic, but people actually have to *decide* to come to the House. They have to make a conscious decision to go get a head of stinky French cheese. There can't be that many pretentious jackasses in the world.

Mike slows his bike a half a block away from the shop, next to the ice cream parlor, because waiting outside the House, presumably for Leoni, is Wallace. He's leaning against the brick with ankles crossed and head tilted down. His dark hair falls over his forehead in messy waves. He's tapping fingers rhythmically on his thigh, and Mike realizes he's got earbuds in. An iPhone wire winds over his chest, disappearing into the left pocket of his jeans.

Wallace is taller than him. He's lean and rangy, like a wolf, with big hands and knobby wrists, and enough leg that Mike isn't sure he's jealous of him or wants to rub one off on his thigh.

Mike's in serious trouble here. *Christ.*

He takes a deep breath and pushes off again on his pedals, breaking at the bike rest in front of the shop so his tires skid a little on the sidewalk.

Wallace glances up at him, eyes widening slightly in

surprise. And then he grins, just this side of sheepish. "Tate," he says.

"Hey," Mike says. His stomach feels like it wants to eat itself. Wow, this is so awkward.

"Yeah, so." Wallace tugs his earbuds out. The tops of his cheeks are a little pink, but Mike isn't sure if it's from the cold or not. "I should probably apologize for—"

Oh, for fuck's sake, Mike definitely doesn't want to hear this. He cuts Wallace off with "Whatever, man, you were drunk, I was drunk, things happened, let's really not do this, okay?"

"I wasn't drunk," Wallace says, a quizzical little wrinkle in his brow that is not at all cute, because he's very obviously a moron and won't take a fucking life buoy even when it hits him in the head.

"Wallace," Mike says, kind of exasperated. He flicks down his kickstand and swings off his bike.

"I just wanted to say sorry for pushing you," Wallace says. "I mean, you didn't really protest." His grin gets sly, one corner of his mouth higher than the other, and Mike kind of wants to slap him. "But I didn't ask, either."

Mike says, "You always ask before you kiss someone?" before he can stop himself.

Wallace takes a step closer to him. "Sure," he says, voice low. His eyes are sparkling.

Mike has no idea why he's still in this conversation.

Wallace is only a couple feet away from Mike, but it

doesn't matter. Mike clenches his hands into fists, feels his heart trip like a fucking traitor, his chest feels hot. He doesn't want to stare at Wallace, but it's not like he has much of a choice. Wallace is like a motherfucking cobra, his gaze is *mesmerizing*. Wallace is messing with him, he knows this, but it's like his dick doesn't care. That's really inconvenient.

His brain is calling for a strategic retreat, though. He says, "I need to get inside," and sidesteps around Wallace, almost barreling into a scowling Leoni in his haste to get through the door.

The first week of November is mostly a blur for Mike. He goes to school, hangs out with the guys, and works, but he can't actually recall any of it in clear detail.

"You're acting weird," Cam says to Mike at lunch on Friday.

Mike is totally acting weird. He's not even surprised that Cam has noticed this. Still, he says, "No, I'm not."

Cam leans his elbows onto the table, eyes narrowed. "You are, man. You're acting like that time, that time you ate bad chicken and had the shits for a week."

Cam is so classy. Mike's glad they're friends.

"Could we not talk about that while we're eating lunch?" Meckles says, grimacing.

"Or at all," Mike says. "We could try that."

Cam keeps staring at Mike. He says, "You're going to have to tell me eventually, dude. I'm your best friend."

Mike stares back. "You really want to know?"

"Yes, Mike," Cam says. "Yes, I want to know why you're acting so fucking *weird*."

Cam is rarely serious. Even his bouts of seriousness aren't really all that serious. The one time Mike's ever seen Cam truly upset was when his mom died, and they were both seven at the time. Cam is always a little bit crazy—funny hats, fanny packs, fake mustaches, a stuffed badger—and he cracks tasteless jokes when he's being carted off to the hospital, no matter how many broken bones he's got. Every cloud has a sterling silver lining for Cam.

Cam's keeping a straight face now, but it's hard to take him seriously under that ridiculous coonskin cap.

Mike cocks his head. "Are you Davy Crockett today?"

"Killed me a bear when I was only three."

"Mike's deflecting," Jason says.

"And you're an asshole," Mike says. Jay knows better than anyone, except maybe Lisa, why Mike is acting so weird. Besides the whole kissing Wallace thing, which no one will ever know about ever, Mike has decided.

"Mike," Cam says sternly, and here, right now, Mike thinks he could totally do it. It's just them, just Cam and Meckles and Jay—his closest friends. He could totally come out.

Omar sits down next to Cam and says, "What's up?"

Omar. Omar would get it, Mike knows this. Omar's probably the only one he's absolutely sure about. Mike could say, *You know that nothing? From before? Well, that nothing is a big gay queer,* and Mike's totally sure it'll be awesome and fine and they would all go back to eating their lunches like nothing happened. Right.

Jason frowns at him.

"I'm being weird about Homecoming, all right?" Mike says, like a lying liar who lies.

"Well, *duh,*" Cam says. "It's like you're the star of every eighties teen movie ever." He smiles dreamily. "I wish I could be you."

Sometimes, Mike has no idea what's going on in Cam's brain. Or rather, he knows exactly what's going on in there. He just doesn't want to think about it.

"Now," Cam says, waggling his eyebrows, "have you thought about your royal escort?"

"I'm going stag," Mike says.

Jason says, "Lisa will destroy you," because he's apparently making it his mission to stomp all over Mike's fragile hopes and dreams.

Mike glares at him.

Jason just smiles, like Mike *won't* kick his ass. Which he won't. Because Mike is a fucking pansy who loves his friends, goddamn it.

And then Omar, who is the best of them—the *best,* despite getting completely trashed at Cam's Halloween party and throwing up all over Lenny's hooker boots—changes the subject, and Mike is saved from having to explain that, yes, he kind of wants his *royal escort* to have a cock and big hands.

Those things are better left unsaid.

For three years, Wallace has been in the same science classes as Mike. For the past two, they've been in the same English classes, too. It's not like Mike hasn't *noticed* this before, it's just that now he's much more aware of Wallace's location in relation to himself.

"What's up your ass?" Mo says.

Mike hunches his shoulders. The hairs on the back of his neck are prickling, but he refuses to look up and confirm that Wallace is staring at him again from across the room. "Nothing," he says, then leans toward her and hisses, "Wallace is stalking me," because he has to tell *someone*. Someone who will probably not make fun of him, like Cam or Meckles.

Mo blinks. "You're delusional. And paranoid."

Mike shakes his head. Obviously not Mo, either. "Shut up."

"You—you know what, whatever." She grins at him. "You're just freaking out about Homecoming."

"Hell, yeah," he says, happy to steer the conversation away from Wallace.

"I'm thinking about skipping out on it. Wanna join me?"

"Lisa would cut off my balls and put them in a jar. So no," Mike says. He *yearns* to skip out on Homecoming, but it isn't worth it.

"Okay." She frowns down at her desk, and Mike curses his tender heart.

He sighs. "Okay, what?"

Mo sucks in her bottom lip, teeth closing over her two lip rings. Her eyes are dark, and her fingers are fidgeting with her pen—there's a blue ink smudge on the inside of her right thumb. "It's just—the nomination's gotta be someone's sick idea of a joke. Look at me."

Mike looks at her. The tips of her pixie cut are currently dyed red. She's got thick black around her eyes, a barbell that cuts across her left eyebrow, and the ends of a black-and-red tattoo curving up over the back of her neck. Mike gets what she's saying, but at the same time he doesn't. "Mo, seriously, this isn't *Carrie*. You realize your best friend is Dorothy Ramirez, right?"

Even if it'd started out as a joke, which is possible, because they've got the requisite asswipes in their class who think they're better than everyone else—the junior varsity football players, the jockette clones on the field hockey team, the Mandees, none of whom are actually named Mandee—Dotty wouldn't let anything happen.

But Mo just shrugs.

"You know what you should do?" Mike says.

"What?"

"You should own it." Mike has no idea what he's doing. Mike has no business telling anyone to own anything, considering the mess that is currently his life, but as long as he's doing this, he doesn't have to think about Wallace or making out with guys. That's a plus right now.

One of Mo's eyes squints a little in question. "Own what, exactly?"

"Homecoming. Don't let anyone make you feel uncomfortable, Mo. Get yourself a date and go and be awesome."

"Right," Mo says. She's looking at him like he's grown three other heads, and he doesn't blame her. He knows he sounds like a tool.

"In fact," Mike makes himself go on, "you should ask Jeremy Smith."

"Jeremy—are you *high*?"

"Nope." He just really, really wishes he were.

"Smith's a *mathlete*."

Mike says, "He likes you."

Mo's still watching him like he's some sort of alien or werewolf or hybrid robot dog-beast. Which is fitting, since Mike's pretty sure Smith's in the Paranormal Enthusiasts club.

"Smith," she says.

"Jeremy Smith," Mike says with a nod.

Mo gives him another weird look before opening *Hamlet* and toying with the dog-eared corner of a page.

Up front, Mrs. Saunders is explaining how much of a crazy person Hamlet is, and Mike thinks about how this play is pretty fucked up.

In his peripheral vision, Wallace's face is a blur. When Mike finally glances over, Wallace isn't looking at him, but Mike isn't fooled. The corner of Wallace's mouth is curled, and there's a pink flush across the top of his cheek. Mike's glad one of them is finding this so amusing.

Mo slides a piece of paper onto his desk. On it is: *seriously, smith?*

Mike writes, *yes, smith, just ask him,* and tries not to think about how much he's acting like a giant twelve-year-old girl.

twelve.

Mike has nothing against Wallace's youn-
ger brother, Serge. The kid's pale and weird, and he wears
a studded dog collar, but Mike's best friend owns five different pairs of boat shoes, so Mike doesn't have any room to
talk.

Not only does he have nothing against Serge, he kind of
feels sorry for him. It's gotta be tough, living in your brother's
perfect shadow. Serge takes it like an emo kid, not a man,
but he's fourteen and a frosh. Allowances have to be made.

So Mike's understandably concerned when he sees Serge
in the hallway after lunch on Monday, sporting a fist-shaped
red mark on his face and a split lower lip. Huh.

Wallace is standing next to him, frowning with worry,
and Serge has a defensive tilt to his chin, even though his
eyes look suspiciously wet.

Mike feels something clench in his rib cage.

They actually look a lot alike, even though Serge is
shorter and thinner. There's a resemblance when they're
apart, but standing together Mike can see how their noses

match, and how many times the expressions on their faces mirror each other as they talk.

They're both pissed off, just for two different reasons.

And then Mike realizes he's staring and turns away.

Mike might be in an epic battle of wills with Wallace, but that doesn't mean he can't do anything when he spots a couple sophomores roughing Serge up on his way home from school later in the week.

"Pull over," Mike tells Omar.

Omar arches an eyebrow, but obediently pulls onto the side of the road, leaving the van idling. He sits there while Mike pops open the passenger door.

"Well?" Mike says, looking back at him. "Aren't you going to help?"

Omar sighs and twists off the engine. "You're going to get your ass kicked."

"No way, man, I'm a ninja," Mike says, grinning. With Omar, it'll be three against two—although, honestly, it looks like Serge won't be much of a help, poor kid, he's not doing a lot to defend himself—and Mike considers himself a pretty scrappy fighter.

Omar huffs a laugh and gets out of the van.

Serge has his book bag tucked protectively against his chest. He's scowling, and there's a smudge of fresh blood on the corner of his mouth. The older bruise on his face is dark purple, yellowing at the edges.

Mike's just close enough to hear one of the assholes say "fucking emo *fag*," and Serge's face goes blank, just shuts down, even though his knuckles are white against the dark fabric of his bag.

Mike says, "Hey, douche bags," hoping to draw them away from Serge.

The second their attention is diverted, Serge kicks one of them in the balls; Mike has seriously underestimated him.

Omar winces. "Ouch."

The kid currently *not* rolling around on the ground crying looks pissed, but also like he wants to run away before Serge can get another lucky shot in.

Mike makes a *c'mere* gesture at Serge, and Serge tightens his jaw, but makes his way cautiously over. Mike says, "Get in. We'll give you a ride."

"I can walk," Serge says.

"Sure you can." Mike nods. "Or you can get in the van and those assholes won't call their friends to jump you five blocks from now."

Serge looks at Omar, and Omar shrugs.

He still seems hesitant, though, and Mike catches his arm and steers him toward the van. "You know me, Serge," he says. "We're just gonna drive you home."

Mike feels some of the tension seep out of Serge's arm. "Okay," he says. "Thanks."

Serge has shadows under his eyes, and he looks more sickly than Goth-pale. This school year has obviously been hard on him so far. He's still got a death grip on his bag as he climbs into the back of the van.

Mike leans into the doorframe and watches Serge settle onto a seat, rubbing absently at his mouth, smearing blood along his jaw, and he's so tense Mike doesn't want to take him home yet. He's got a feeling Serge would just disappear until tomorrow morning, or he'd be hounded by his brother— Wallace doesn't seem like the type of guy who'd really get this kind of bullying. Fortunately, Mike's in a benevolent savior kind of mood. Takes his mind off his own problems.

"Know anything about music?" Mike asks him.

Serge scowls and says, "Maybe."

"Okay." Mike bobs his head. "Wanna hang out with us for a little while?"

Serge says, "Not really."

"Sure you do," Mike says. "You'll love it." He pats the top of the van before pulling the door closed.

Omar grins at him. "Are we kidnapping a freshman?"

"Yes, Omar. Yes, we are."

It takes a while for Serge to relax. For him to really believe that they're not going to beat the shit out of him in the comfort of Meckles' basement.

Serge loosens up enough to agree with Meckles about

Nirvana, even though Meckles is *wrong*. And he accepts Mike's admittedly somewhat shaky reasoning on why the Lemonheads rock: they've written the sound track to Mike's entire life, basically, and Evan Dando is a god. Omar shows him how to play the bass part on "My Drug Buddy," and Serge proves himself a truly terrible musician.

Cam doesn't let Serge smoke up. "Not on my watch, little dude," he says, mainly because Cam's a bitch and a hoarder. But the contact high is enough to leave Serge mellow when they leave. Mike's got a tolerance built up, even with his two months of abstinence, but he's still more relaxed than he's been in a while. He tends to think it's the company more than anything.

Omar drives them back around six, and then Mike walks Serge home, four houses down from his own.

Mike leans into Serge's side, comfortable, and the front door opens before they even make it all the way up the walk.

"What are you doing?" Wallace asks when they hit the front stoop, staring at the arm Mike's got dangling across Serge's shoulders.

"Dropping Serge off," Mike says. He shifts away and gives the middle of Serge's back a push. "Go on, scamp. See you tomorrow."

Serge doesn't smile, but his eyes light up as he glances over at him. He ducks his head and mumbles, "Bye."

Mike stuffs his hands in his pockets, rocks back on his heels and grins, ignoring Wallace's frown. He's not letting

Wallace get him down. They had a killer afternoon, even if Serge thinks death metal is an acceptable musical genre.

With a jaunty wave, Mike sets off across the lawn toward his house.

"Hey," Wallace says.

Mike turns so he's looking at Wallace and slows his steps. "Yeah?"

Wallace just stares at him, mouth pulled down. Finally, he shakes his head and says, "Never mind."

"So what you're saying is that you have a crush on Rook Wallace's fourteen-year-old brother," Lisa says, leaning a hip onto the locker next to Mike's.

"Fuck no," Mike says. "He's just an all right kid." Mike wants to take him under his wing, mentor him, do all the shit Wallace should be doing, but is apparently too busy to do. It's clear to Mike after hanging out with Serge the day before that *someone* has been entirely remiss in schooling Serge on the differences between tragically hip and cool. Mike doesn't care how Serge dresses, so long as he doesn't get his wardrobe from Hot Topic. He should hang out with Girl Meckles.

Lisa looks at him with a skeptical gleam in her eyes. She crosses her arms over her chest. "Really," she says.

"Yes, really."

Sighing, Lisa steps closer and slides a hand over his

forearm. She moves into him, hooking her chin over his shoulder, sort of a half hug. She says, "You know, I kind of miss you."

Mike wraps his other arm around her waist. "No, you don't."

She huffs. "I *do*. We never hang out anymore."

"That's because you have Larson. And I have cheer-leaders."

Lisa chuckles. "It's pretty funny."

"Whatever," Mike grouses. He shifts so his nose is buried in her hair and hugs her tighter. Around them, the hall is mostly empty—the first bell for homeroom's already rung. They should be rushing, but Mike doesn't feel like it.

Finally, Lisa lifts her head and looks right into Mike's eyes and says, "I know you."

"Yeah." There's no way Mike can even try to deny that. Lisa's known Mike as long as Cam has.

"You're avoiding things. You're adopting Serge to avoid even more things." She pokes him in the stomach. "Are you going to tell me what happened at Cam's party?"

"Uh, no," Mike says, and then says, "Crap," when Lisa's expression turns smug. She'd been fishing, and he'd just confirmed her suspicions. He backtracks with, "I mean—what? Nothing happened," but he's not dumb enough to think he's fooled her.

The second homeroom bell rings.

Lisa pokes him again and says, "You're telling me later."

Mike has no intention of telling her anything later, but he nods *okay* anyway.

Health class is a giant waste of time, but Mike only has it once a week. He sits in the back corner in between Omar and Jason, by the bank of windows, and zones out for an hour.

The classroom is one of two in the gym hallway, and the windows are facing the soccer field. It's a nice day for the middle of November, and there's a fifth period gym class out in the sunshine playing croquet. Badly. Mike's pretty sure it's on purpose.

He spots Lenny, hair pulled back in a sleek ponytail, laughing with Wallace. She's got a hand on his arm, head tipped back, grinning, and Mike does not care. He doesn't clench his teeth or tighten his fingers around his pen. That would be stupid.

He's not going to be one of those assholes who decides he doesn't want someone, but gets jealous when that someone wants someone else.

Wallace leans away from Lenny, though. He's smiling, from what Mike can tell, but he deftly maneuvers some space between them, so smooth Mike doesn't think Lenny even notices. Wallace bobs his head in an *aw-shucks* motion, but keeps his croquet club angled out, so Lenny can't move any closer.

Mike frowns. Lenny likes to flirt; even Mike sometimes has a hard time not humoring her. It's not like she's even serious, it's just her default. Wallace is acting like Lenny is making him *uncomfortable*, though. Huh.

This is what Mike knows: Wallace has never had a girl-friend.

Mike tries to think if he's ever even seen Wallace date. He chews on the end of his pen, watching the orange-gold autumn sun somehow make Wallace's black hair even richer looking. Wallace elbows Weedy Jim in the ribs, laughing companionably.

In all those years of heated, evil glances, you'd think Mike would've heard something about a girl. It's not like he even thought it was weird that Wallace didn't date, because then maybe he'd have thought of this sooner: he remembers that guy. That senior, that varsity baseball player, Buschel, from last year, the one that practically adopted Wallace. Mike remembers it being sickening, all the male bonding and back-slaps and blushing cheeks, and Mike's horrified to realize that, yes, Buschel and Wallace had probably been *fucking like bunnies.*

Mike makes a choking noise.

Omar looks at him funny.

Mike coughs into his fist.

Motherfucking shit, he thinks.

So Wallace is most likely really, really gay, huh, and that makes Mike—actually, he has no idea what that makes him. It's practically a confirmation that Wallace is fucking with him, though, like he wants to taunt Mike for being so hesitant about something that Wallace is already so at ease with. Like Mike's *ashamed* instead of just really confused. It makes him feel sick to his stomach, and something suspiciously like hurt settles somewhere heavy in his chest.

Whatever. It's not like Mike was taking any of this seriously anyhow.

And even if eventually, by some small chance, he *would have*, well, he certainly won't now.

"Serge, my man," Mike says. Serge is standing by his brother's Nova in the parking lot while Wallace unlocks it. Mike gives Wallace a tight grin before grabbing Serge's wrist and tugging him toward Omar's van. "Ditch your brother and come with us."

"Serge," Wallace says. Mike can hear the frown in his voice, even with his back to him.

"We're heading to the Lot," Mike says to Serge. "Cam's promised me a death-defying feat. You don't want to miss it."

"I guess," Serge says. He says it reluctantly, but Mike can totally see a twinkle in his eye. Mike's on a mission. A mission to shake Serge out of his funk; all this punk-ass emo shit is lame. Goth, fine, Mike can take it—he takes Meckles' lumberjack and Cam's stupid surfer, he can handle black,

black, and yet even more black—but there's no law that says a Goth can't have fun.

"Serge," Wallace says louder.

Mike looks over his shoulder at him. "Don't worry, Wallace, we'll keep your bro safe."

Wallace is scowling. Mike doesn't think he's ever seen his mouth curve down quite so hard before.

It makes Mike feel strangely giddy. He's not *using* Serge by befriending him, exactly; finally pissing Wallace off is just a nice added perk.

The Lot is busy for a weeknight, probably because it's so nice out. And also because Cam's got a megaphone—who the hell knows *how*—and is loudly proclaiming his intentions of jumping his bike over Omar's van. It's not the wildest thing he's ever done, but it's up there with the stupidest. Nobody is bothering to try to talk him out of it, not even Deanna. She's got a look on her face like she's fed up and mostly amused, like maybe letting Cam do this will make him tame for the rest of the year.

It's a nice thought. False, but nice.

There's a ramp—it's not so much curved as warped— made out of pieces of plywood; Mike's not sure where Cam got them, but they look almost rotted through. At least Cam's wearing a helmet. Usually, they have to fight him on that.

"Ladies and gentlemen," Cam says with a flourish, half on his dirt bike, one hand in the air. "Let's fucking do this."

Serge says, slight awe in his voice, "Is he trying to kill himself?"

"You'd think so, right?" Mike says, grinning. Cam is a crazy bastard.

It's almost dark out, early twilight. Mike can see his breath. They're loud, all of them, and someone nearby has probably already called the cops. Still, they haven't gotten there by the time Cam starts pedaling across the asphalt, or when he hits the shaky ramp that barely holds his weight, or when he tumbles headlong and hard onto Omar's van. He *almost* makes it. There's a single moment where Mike thinks he's actually going to catch enough air to at least roll over the roof. But then his front wheel hits the top corner and Cam flips over onto his back, slamming into the luggage rack and then careening off the other side.

"Hot damn," Cam says, panting and nearly breathless, when Mike reaches his side. "Son of a bitch. *Ow.*" He's grinning maniacally and holding his arm awkwardly against his chest.

"Hospital," Mike says.

"I can shake it off," Cam says. There's some strain around his eyes, though, and he's steadily turning pale gray.

"Hospital," Deanna says, resigned.

"You're lucky you didn't break your head," Omar says.

Jason has his cell phone up to his ear. He says brightly, "Hi, Mr. Scott," and Mike starts helping Cam to his feet.

Mike has no idea what time it is when Omar finally drops him and Serge off, but it's late. They'd gone to the hospital with Cam, waited for his dad to show up, and then gone for milk shakes with Omar and Jay.

All the stars are as bright as the moon, and the air is crisp and frigid. Mike has his hands stuffed in the front pocket of his hoodie as he walks Serge home. He's not even sure why he does it, why he feels like he has to make sure Serge actually gets to his front door, but it could be the way Wallace opens it before they reach it—*again*—and how he still looks angry.

Wallace says, "You're late." His arms are crossed, and his gaze bounces hotly between them.

"Sorry, Wallace," Mike says insincerely. "Didn't realize the kid had a curfew."

"I don't," Serge says, glaring at his brother.

Mike claps his shoulder. He's getting a really nice sense of satisfaction in annoying Wallace, since it's kind of amazingly shitty that Wallace can kick his ass when they're twelve and then kiss him all these years later with absolutely no explanation or apology. Mike's spent so many years raging against Wallace, while Wallace never even got *flustered*—just smiled at Mike like he was someone's

152

amusing pet monkey. And now there's something in Wallace's eyes that Mike's never seen before, and it warms Mike right down to his soul. This is Mike, finally gaining the upper hand. This is Mike: triumphant.

He grins up at Wallace, tips his head back, and stares him right in the face.

Wallace works his mouth like he wants to say something, but nothing comes out.

Serge says, "It's not even ten, *god*," and pushes past Wallace to get inside.

"Things happened beyond my control, Wallace," Mike says. He feels like he's being gracious here, offering an explanation.

Wallace remains silent and continues to try to burn a hole through Mike's head with his eyes.

Mike nods. "Right." While there's fun in making Wallace speechless, he thinks it'd be better if he could get Wallace to yell at him—he's not going to examine *why* it would be better—and now they're just staring at each other, a silent standoff.

When Wallace eases up on his frown and licks his lips, Mike's mind goes from zero to sixty in a direction he totally doesn't want it to go. Right.

Mike's just going to get out of there while he's still ahead.

thirteen.

Cam's stunt leaves him with a dislocated shoulder and a broken wrist. Mike thinks he got off easy, considering the way he'd landed.

No one's all that sympathetic, because he's still alive and with no permanent damage, and also, Cam doesn't really *invite* sympathy. Cam wants people to remember the stunt, the sick way his bike flipped, the hollow thud of him hitting the roof. He goes over the shaky cell-phone video of it, pointing out all the little details with giddy relish and self-satisfaction.

Cam and Deanna have a fight about it and break up for exactly one day. They make up, mainly because Cam isn't going to change, and because Mike thinks Deanna doesn't really want him to.

Despite being injured, Cam doesn't use this as an excuse to get out of the Homecoming dance. Mike's caught between being relieved and horrified, because he knows Cam just wants to go and watch Mike humiliate himself, but it'll still be nice to have his friends there. They've been at the mall for almost two hours, though, and Mike kind of wants to jab an ice pick through his brain. He only agreed to shop with Cam because the alternative was shopping with Lisa. He's starting to think that actually would've been easier.

Cam tells Mike, "You can't actually go stag, you know that, right? Everyone will totally think you're boning Jay."

Mike blinks. He doesn't even flush, because there are so many things wrong with that sentence—so crazy it's not even embarrassing. "No they won't," he says.

"Two dudes going stag with a bunch of other couples equals gay," Cam says. He holds up a pink-and-green striped shirt with his good arm. "What do you think?"

"I think—" Mike thinks that maybe it *is* gay, but also maybe that it doesn't matter. He shakes his head. "I don't think anyone would think I was dating Jason. Dude's too skinny."

Cam doesn't even give him a weird look; he just nods his head. "True that." He picks up another green shirt and adds it to his pile to try on. Mike has a packaged white shirt and a dark blue tie. He hates shopping.

"Isn't your suit navy?" Mike says.

"You're right, I should go for something yellow," Cam says, then starts back down the row of dress shirts.

"Anyway," Mike says, trailing reluctantly after Cam, "what about Omar?"

"Omar has a date."

"*Omar* has a date?"

"You should be more surprised that Meckles has a

date," Cam says, flipping through novelty ties. Mike catches glimpses of turkeys and cornucopias.

This is true, except Mike's mainly responsible for Meckles' date. He's 99 percent sure Dotty did the asking, too, and he's looking forward to the inevitable and hilarious panic attack Meckles'll have day of.

But Omar is just *Omar*. He's not like Meckles; Mike just can't picture him taking time out of his busy schedule of being absently wise and terminally laid-back to suffer through the teen awkwardness of *dating*. He just figured Omar would wake up one day married with three kids. Like magic.

"Who is it?" Mike asks.

Cam looks over and waggles his eyebrows. "Fitzsimmons."

"Jules? He's taking *Jules* Fitzsimmons?"

"Well, I doubt he's taking Gabe Fitzsimmons," Cam says, frowning at what looks like a solar system tie.

"Huh." Jules Fitzsimmons is a control freak, but her older brother's a nut job. He has dead eyes and a penchant for staring. Even Cam thinks he's out of his mind, and Mike knows Lisa—*Lisa*, hardened soul, Viking—is a little afraid of him, so he has a point.

"I think I'm going about this the wrong way," Cam says. "I'm pretty sure I can pull off a bolo. I'll get a brown suit and cowboy boots, like I stepped out of *Dallas* and into Dee's dreams."

Mike doesn't say anything, even though he thinks it's the

worst idea ever and that there's a strong chance Girl Meckles will kick his ass over it. Deanna's being an actual girl about Homecoming; she's getting her hair and makeup done with Lisa and everything.

Mike doesn't say anything, though. Half because he doesn't want to encourage Cam and half because he knows it won't matter what he says, anyhow.

Sometime in between their kiss and Mike doing everything possible to convince himself he doesn't give a shit about Wallace, something happens: Wallace stops giving a shit about *him*.

The last committee meeting for Homecoming, only five days before the actual dance, is weird. Mike gets the distinct feeling Wallace is freezing him out. No doubt he's angry that Mike's hanging out with Serge, because at some point Cam's going to talk Serge into doing something stupid or dangerous, or stupid *and* dangerous; that's a given. And Mike's not sure why it bothers him, either, but Wallace is giving him cool looks and polite smiles and Mike never thought he'd miss Devil Incarnate Wallace, the smirks and odd attentiveness and innately evil soul. But it does bother him. It really, really does.

Mike spends the whole meeting staring at Wallace without really staring at him. Tragically, he doesn't even think Wallace notices.

"So why does Rook suddenly have a massive stick up his ass?" Dotty asks, stalking him to his locker after the meeting.

"How the fuck would I know?" Mike says, disgruntled. Fingers fumbling, it takes him three tries to spin the lock and get it open.

Dotty stares at him with narrowed eyes. She says, "Maybe because he's only acting like this around *you*."

Mike bites his lip and tugs his jacket out of his locker before slamming it closed again. "That doesn't mean anything."

"It means you had a fight," Dotty says, and what the fuck, how does she get *that* out of this, when Mike and Wallace have never ever been friends to begin with?

Is it Mike's fault that his archnemesis has devolved into fucking *pouting* in his presence? Or, like, being coolly disdainful, whatever. Mike still doesn't get how befriending Serge has turned into this mess.

Mike clenches his hands into the thick canvas sleeves of his army jacket. He feels like it would be so much easier to accept this and move on if Wallace hadn't manhandled him like a cheap whore at Cam's Halloween party. That part, he's willing to admit, he'd liked a little too much. And because of that, all the rest of this shit is pissing him off.

But it's just like with J. J. *It was just a kiss.* Right?

Dotty squeezes his arm. "Mike?"

Mike rolls his shoulders, dislodging her hand. He slips on his coat and says, "Yeah, no, I'm okay."

Mike is miserable for the rest of the week. It's pathetic, but he can't help it, everything just feels *wrong*. Off-kilter.

Friday afternoon, he spends the pep rally underneath the gym bleachers. He sits propped up against a metal support beam, knees bent, dust all over his jeans, and listens to the band swell in between announcing the starting varsity football players. When they start on the Junior and Royal Courts, Mike holds his breath, hands balled into fists over his kneecaps, but they take his absence in stride. He smiles a little when they call Mo's name along with Smith's. So there's Mo, shoving it in everyone's faces. She's a brave little toaster.

"Thought I'd find you under here."

Mike tilts his head back to look up at Cam. Cam's forearm cast is completely covered in multicolored writing and obscene pictures. "Where's your sling?"

"Fuck my sling," Cam says. "I'm fine."

Cam definitely isn't *fine*, but he's always had a ridiculously high tolerance for pain, so whatever. His shoulder must still hurt like a bitch, especially with the weight of the cast, but if Cam can take it, Mike's not gonna be a mom about it. That's what Cam has Deanna for.

Cam drops down onto the ground next to him, wincing a

little when he jars his arm. They sit quietly when the band starts up again—since it's not like they could hear each other over it, anyway. Mike's only somewhat cheered by their Daft Punk medley. Mike hates Daft Punk, but everything sounds better with crazy amounts of percussion.

Mike and Cam have been friends since preschool. Mike doesn't remember meeting him—or Lisa, either. All three of them ended up in the same classroom, but his mom says he came home from his very first day talking nonstop about a boy in a Spider-Man shirt and red pants, and they've been inseparable ever since. They've been picked up by the police no less than five times over the years, most often for Cam's stupid stunts, but that one time for public nudity, which sadly had nothing to do with alcohol at all. Their families take vacations together, spend holidays together, hold joint barbecues. There was a time when Mike had wished Uncle Jem and his mom would just get married already. And even though that's never happened—and isn't ever going to happen, since Mom's likened it to incest—they're still some sort of mishmashed family, anyway.

Mike has known Cam the *longest*. Longer than Meckles and Deanna, who they both knew since second grade, and longer than Omar, who they met the first week of middle school.

Mike should be able to tell Cam anything.

Deep breath . . .

Mike nudges Cam's sneaker with his own. "So," he says

in the short lull between songs and cheers. "I'm pretty sure I like guys."

He feels Cam tense for a long moment, all along his side, and Mike's stomach flips over.

Then Cam says, "Sexual deviancy, dude. I totally approve."

Mike chokes out a laugh. "Fuck you," he says, and he goes almost boneless with relief.

Cam jostles his arm and says, "You know, that conversation about Tobey Maguire makes a lot more sense now."

The football game is a disaster, as most of their football games are. They have no hope of winning, that's obvious five minutes in. Then it starts raining halfway through the second quarter, the band gives up the ghost, and Mike happily retreats to Omar's van.

This is where he's accosted by Lisa. She swoops out of nowhere, her long dark hair plastered to her skull, water dripping off the end of her nose, face scary-pale from the cold rain. Mike barely manages to stifle a yelp of terror when she grabs his arm.

"I'm letting you go stag," Lisa says, pushing him across the bench seat as she follows him into the back of the van, "but I'm certainly not letting you dress yourself."

"I have a suit," Mike says defensively. He actually has two suits to choose from. He knows what's *appropriate*, thanks very much. "I'm not Cam."

"Cam has a suit, too," Lisa says, unimpressed. "I'm sure he'll show up with a tequila sunrise shirt tucked into his slacks. That's not my problem. You're my problem."

"Hey, I stopped being your problem a couple months ago." He doesn't *mean* to sound petulant, but he's cold and wet and he has to go to a *school dance* tomorrow night, and he's not Lisa's anything now.

"Oh, Michael," she says, reaching over, sodden hoodie and all, and squishing him into a hug. Mike's face is mashed into her soaked shoulder, but it's not like he could get any wetter. "You'll *always* be my problem."

Mike tries to pretend like he isn't melting inside— Lisa's like a sharp-toothed wolverine with unexpected soft spots. He snakes his arms around her waist and pulls her closer.

"I'm reluctantly impressed," Lisa says.

"Thanks," Mike says dryly.

Mike has a black suit from last Christmas and a gunmetal gray one his mom made him get for this past Easter. He has no preference for either of them, but he figured he'd wear the black. He doesn't think he can go wrong with black for evening wear.

Lisa pulls out the gray one, though. "Let's see your ties," she says.

Mike has the navy tie he bought with Cam, a diamond-patterned champagne one with some unidentifiable stain on it, and a plain deep red one that's only a little creased.

"Red," Lisa says, nose wrinkled. "I'll iron it for you." She tosses it onto his bed, then places her hands on her hips and stares at him.

Mike lasts for a full minute before caving with an unfortunately whiny "What?"

"You know what," she says.

"Not sure I do," Mike says, even though he's blatantly *lying*. Damn it. He was really hoping she'd forget about the whole Halloween party thing.

"Spill." Lisa's eyes are scary-narrow and her toes start tapping impatiently. Mike would ignore these warning signs if he didn't suspect that they'd lead to painful maiming and/or public humiliation.

So Mike says, "Wallace kissed me." He's downplaying it a little, of course, because what Wallace really did was attack his face and use his tongue for sexy evil, but he doesn't want to get into those specifics with Lisa.

"Oh my god," she says. A wide grin breaks across her face and she punches him in the arm. "I *knew* it!"

Mike flinches away, frowning. "Knew what?"

"Rook! Rook has—wait." Lisa pauses, waving a hand. "We *are* talking about Rook, right, not Serge?"

"Uh, yeah." Mike makes a face. It would be really weird

and kind of gross if Serge kissed him. No offense to Serge; he's just way too young and, uh, pale.

"*Yes.*" Lisa pokes him this time, hard in the chest; Mike's going to have bruises later. "Rook has a crush on you. Or more than a crush, I can't decide." She shrugs. "Whatever, Rook *likes* you, I know he does."

"Wallace likes everyone. It's his cover for being the Antichrist." Mike knows he's being unfair, but Wallace has been on his hate list for so long that this response is kind of knee-jerk for him.

Lisa looks disappointed. "Michael."

Mike drops down onto the edge of his bed. "I don't know what it is, but Wallace doesn't have a crush on me. We're not even talking." Not like they normally talk, but that's the only way he can think of to describe how Wallace is pointedly denying his existence at the moment.

"What do you mean you *don't know*? Are we talking making-out kissing, or, like, a peck on the cheek?" Lisa says.

Mike feels his face get hot. "Um."

"Oh my *god*, seriously." Lisa sits down next to him, hand gripping his leg just above the knee. "Was it better than J. J.? Tell me it was better than J. J."

"I don't remember J. J.," Mike mutters. He flops back, sprawling out on the bed, arms wide. He's not sure how to describe Wallace's kiss without gushing about how hot it was. He really doesn't want to have this conversation with Lisa. "It was . . . nice."

"Nice," Lisa says, skeptical. She turns a little, pulling a leg up to curl on the mattress so she can stare into his soul.

Mike sighs and presses his palms into his eye sockets. "I might have climbed him like a monkey. I was wearing a *skirt*, Lisa."

"Right." Lisa grabs hold of his thigh again. "Right, start from the beginning."

Mike lifts one hand and peeks out at her. She looks disturbingly gleeful, even though she's not actually smiling. "He asked about me and J. J., I told him to mind his own business." Close enough. "He kissed me, and now here we are."

The corners of her mouth pull down. "There has to be more to it than that," she says.

"Considering the cold shoulder he's giving me? I think there's even *less* to it than that." And Mike is totally not bitter or disappointed about that.

Lisa slumps. She digs her elbow into her knee and drops her chin into her palm. "Huh."

"Yeah." He stares up at his ceiling. His body feels sleep-heavy, tired. He wants to crawl into a dark hole and stay there for a week or three. Then maybe the world as he knows it will start making sense again. Christ, being an angsty, emo teen is fucking *exhausting*.

If he had any energy left at all he'd kick his own ass for being such a pussy.

fourteen.

Mike wakes up Saturday morning to a knot of dread twisting up his stomach and also to Rosie and her hermit crabs. She's made a hermit crab town out of Play-Doh on his bedroom floor. She's also got every Matchbox car ever made spread out around her and he's got to wonder how long she's been down there. His phone says it's quarter to eleven.

Rosie looks up from where she's trying to stuff poor Godzilla into a rapidly caving-in red-and-yellow house. She says, "Mom says I can get a gecko."

A gecko. Just what they need, a speedy lizard that'll disappear somewhere in the house for Mike to find months later, a dried-out lizard husk. Considering how attached Rosie is to 'Zilla and the Professor, Mike's really not looking forward to that.

Mike slips out from under the covers and onto the rug with a slightly pained oomph as all his limbs hit the floor, then drags himself up and knee-walks over to Rosie, pushing tiny cars out of the way. He says, "What about these guys?" He yawns and picks up Professor Cheese, smiling as his pincers slide out, feelers flicking the air.

Rosie presses her lips together, like she's really thinking hard about it. Then she says, "I'd still love them best."

Mike says, "Rock on," because he's not exactly all the way awake yet. Rosie doesn't care. One of the many reasons why she's so great.

He spends the next hour or so letting Rosie tell him what to do with the hermit crabs, the Play-Doh, the cars, the lone, naked Barbie that mysteriously ended up under Mike's bed. It's mindless and easy, and he doesn't have to think about anything else for however long Rosie has him trapped there.

Which is basically until she decides that Sandwich is hungry. Mike's pretty hungry, too, so he's not complaining, even though he has to scrape his ass off the floor and actually get dressed.

The knot of dread lasts through grilled ham and cheeses and three episodes of *SpongeBob*, and it swells up to clog his throat right around the time there's a knock on the front door. Mike knows *why* the dread's steadily churning into a big ball of vomit: it's four in the afternoon, and it's getting closer and closer to when he'll have to suit up and suffer through a horrifically long night of techno dance tunes.

What he doesn't know is why Serge is on his front stoop, shifting uncomfortably on his feet, hands in his pockets, head bowed. Mike's surprised enough to say, "What are you doing here?" instead of *hi*, but at least it doesn't come out as rude as it could have been.

Serge shrugs. He says, "Rook's being an asshole," to Mike's front stoop.

Mike says, "Yeah, well," with the clear implication that Wallace is an asshole, so yes, that's his natural state, Mike's not exactly shocked. He pulls the door open wider and says, "Come on in, we're watching *iCarly* reruns."

Serge's eyebrows go up.

"Yeah, whatever, like Teeny doesn't make you play with My Little Ponies," Mike says. Mike thanks the god of little sisters everywhere that Rosie would rather play with earthworms than baby dolls, but he'd bet money that Teeny probably has tea parties and that Serge lets her do his makeup.

Serge shrugs again, but the corners of his mouth curve up into something like a smile.

By six, Lisa has called him ten times—to make sure he wears the red tie and his black shoes and that he actually shows up, because if he doesn't she assures him she will hunt him down and beat him to death with his own arm. Omar's also texted to tell him they'll be by around eight to pick him up. Mike doesn't respond to either of them. He just wants everyone to fuck off and die.

He slumps back on his bed and pointedly doesn't look at the clothes Lisa hung on the outside of his closet door.

Serge is sitting on the floor by Mike's stereo, flipping through his DVDs.

Serge gets talky when he's relaxed. Usually it's the opposite for people, like they babble when they're nervous, but Serge shuts down when he's uncomfortable, Mike has noticed, and Serge has been lecturing him on contemporary artists or poets or shoes or something for the past forty minutes. Mike had stopped listening comprehensively at some point, it's all just *blah, blah, blah, Gioia, blah, Nelson, blah, blah, I hate Ginsberg, blah, fight for your right to party—*

"Wait, wait," Mike says, leveraging up on his elbows. When did this evolve into a conversation about the Beastie Boys? "*Licensed to Ill* is an okay album." Mike's never really been into rap, but he's pretty sure everyone's required to like "Sabotage." "But it's not, like—listening to that, it's nothing like hearing Weezer's blue album for the first time." Mike's not talking Hallelujah Chorus or whatever, but that CD blew Mike away when Zack first made him listen to it.

Serge rolls his eyes. "Everyone likes the blue album."

"You say that like that's a bad thing," Mike says. He doesn't get this thing where you can't like what you like because it's popular and gets radio play and is fucking awesome. There's underrated cool, sure, and there's stuff out there that's mind-bogglingly bad, but it's like . . . it's like . . . "Does anyone hate *Flood*? It's physically impossible to hate They Might Be Giants' *Flood*, right?"

"I don't know," Serge says with a frown.

"Trust me," Mike says. "*Flood* is perfection. The blue album rocks. You tap your toes to MisterWives, I know you do, and if you say you don't, you're a fucking liar."

Serge frowns harder, but it doesn't match his eyes. "I don't," he says. "I like Atreyu. Or, like, Cannibal Corpse."

"Dude, you like Cannibal Corpse?" Cannibal Corpse is *gross*. Mike honestly can't see Serge rocking out to them. "I bet you secretly dance all around your basement to Zolof the Rock & Roll Destroyer."

Serge scrunches his face up in disgust. It's fucking *adorable*.

"That's it." Mike laughs. "Come on, you're coming with us to the dance. My black suit should fit you." The minute he says it the lump of sticky shit sitting at the base of his throat starts dissolving. If he can't be happy, at least someone else will be able to share in his misery. It's the best idea Mike's ever had.

"Uh, *no*," Serge says, very obviously horrified.

"You don't have a choice, my friend," he says. There's a good chance this'll piss Wallace off, and a tiny part of Mike is looking forward to it. It's better than being ignored, right?

A flush starts up from Serge's neck, mottling his pale skin—Mike realizes Serge is *pleased*. It's both gratifying and tragic, because Serge should have kids his own age to hang out with, guys who'll appreciate him.

For the first time ever, Mike wishes he were involved in some clubs that spanned grade levels. Maybe he can get Lisa to take Serge with her to drama. He doesn't seem like the kind of kid who'd enjoy a pickup game of baseball.

Although that doesn't mean Mike isn't going to badger him into occasionally playing, anyway, because Serge is kind of great, bad music choices aside, and if no one else will take him, Mike is perfectly willing to keep Serge himself.

While Mike dutifully dresses in the gray suit Lisa chose for him, Serge goes home to take a shower. Mike doesn't know what he tells his parents or siblings, but he comes back looking surprisingly dapper in Mike's black suit, his face still flushed.

Meckles calls Mike at seven thirty and hyperventilates into his phone like a crazy person. This makes Mike feel ten times better about the evening ahead.

Mom makes an appearance right around when they're supposed to leave. She loiters in the doorway to the den and says, "Don't you boys look handsome," and, "It's good to see you, Serge," and, "I'd take pictures, but I know Michael would never forgive me."

Mike says, *"Mom,"* but all she does is laugh.

And then it hits Mike that there's a good possibility that his mom might think Serge is his *date*, and Mike is frozen in terror for all of two minutes—that feel like at least twenty—while the white noise in his head drowns out whatever small talk Serge is surreally engaging in with his mom. It's like his worst nightmare, right up there with Homecoming committee and being gay, so yeah, why *not* this?

When Omar honks the van horn and Mike's jolted out of his catatonia, he grabs Serge's arm and hauls ass out the front door.

Mike's mom just shouts, "Have fun!" after them, and Mike resists the urge to yell *It's not a date!* back in her face, because she'd probably take that as confirmation.

Omar glances at them in the rearview mirror when they climb in the back, one eyebrow arched.

Jules half turns from the passenger seat and says, "We're sneaking in a lowerclassman? How old are you, kid, twelve?"

Serge looks torn between snapping at her and sinking down into the footwell and disappearing. Serge kicks his foot into the back of Omar's seat and mumbles, "Shut up."

Jules laughs. She looks nice, Mike thinks—less starched. Her hair is even down, falling softly over her shoulders. Omar smiles over at her, like she's charming or adorable or something, and it's just too damn weird.

Luckily, it only takes ten minutes to drive to the high school from Mike's house, and half of that is spent air guitaring to "Pinball Wizard," which actually makes Serge laugh.

The plan, Mike thinks as he gets out of the van, is to be in and out. Mike isn't sure about anyone else, but he doesn't want to hang around the whole night. He'll call his mom for a ride if he has to. He tugs on the front of his jacket, the hems of his sleeves, and tries to look more comfortable than he feels.

The music is deafening, even before they open the inner gym doors.

Naomi, one of the seniors from Homecoming committee, bears down on him as soon as they enter. She's got on a hideous neon pink minidress, gold stiletto heels, and says, "You're late, Tate. You need to be announced," in this really pissy voice. She looks like she wants to smack him with her clipboard.

"I need to be what?"

She gives him a long-suffering, almost-disgusted sigh. Naomi has never really liked Mike, so she's probably horrified that Mike's even on the docket. Hell, Mike is, too. "Announced," she repeats. She overpronounces the word, drawing it out in a hiss like the poisonous viper she is. "You're after Rook and Sierra, okay?"

She takes his shoulder and prods him along the gym floor, positioning him at the bottom of the side steps going up to the temporary stage. She narrows her eyes and says, "Stay."

Mike frowns and murmurs, "Why am I even here?" as Naomi wanders off. He means it rhetorically, but Dotty sneaks up behind him and says, "Because of us."

"What?"

"Us," Dotty says. She leans into his arm, hooks a thumb over toward where Lenny is making eyes at some dude who Mike's pretty sure isn't her date. "We totally nominated you. Me and Lenny and Rook."

"What?" Mike can't fucking *believe* this. "This is all your fault!" Cheerleaders are evil. He's not sure whether he's impressed or pissed.

"Oh, come on. We figured it'd be cool, you're our committee rep." She tips her head up and gives him a winning smile. It's the kind of smile that's both mocking and sweet. Dotty's a total asshole.

"I don't give a crap about Homecoming and you know it," Mike says, but he mostly sounds defeated, and maybe a little amused. Dotty has a smug look on her face, and what the hell, everything's already done, anyway. It's not like he can change it. Mike is getting used to feeling out of control. He's not sure if that's a good thing or not.

Dotty reaches up to straighten his tie.

Mike smacks her hands away. He doesn't need to be *groomed*. He straightens his own tie, then turns and notices Wallace a couple steps up from him, pointedly not looking at him. Mike just *knows* it's on purpose.

Wallace's Homecoming escort is Sierra Montoya, which is the stupidest name for a real person in the entire universe. She's also *stunning*. And Mike can't believe he even said that word in his head, but it's so true. Wallace and Sierra are a matching pair in black, their dark heads tilted together, and Mike has the irrational urge to grab hold of Sierra's sleek bob of hair and *yank*. Just—take her down like a puma culling a caribou. He curls his hands into fists, jagged nails digging into his palms, and starts up an inner monologue on all the reasons he does *not* want to be Wallace's pretty, pretty princess instead.

One: Wallace is the devil.

Two: Wallace will, ultimately, laugh at him. That's the kicker. That's the hump Mike can't get over, even if he was willing to play whatever game Wallace had started on Halloween.

"Hey." Meckles knocks Mike's arm with his elbow.

Mike glances up at him. Meckles looks almost relaxed, which means Cam probably caught him for a smoke before they came inside. "You good?" Mike asks.

Meckles says, "Yeah, sure." His face is flushed, but he's smiling. "You?"

They're about to be announced like debutantes to a room full of their peers. Mike wouldn't exactly call that good. Mo and Smith look like they're lining up to get pushed off a cliff. Mike kind of feels the same way.

He shrugs and says, "Fine." He actually has no idea how this is supposed to play out. There must have been King and Queen voting, but fuck if he remembers that. He's planning on being far, far away from here by then.

Meckles claps him on the back, and Mike stumbles into Wallace and there are a few incredibly awkward seconds while they sort out all their limbs, and Mike tries very hard not to grope Wallace or fall on his face and he's so fucking *embarrassed* that the next moments as he's announced are a blur. One second he's waiting on stage, Wallace's big hands steadying him . . .

The next second, he's already back down on the gym floor with Serge and Jay and Omar and Meckles crowded around him. Jason pushes a cup of punch into his hands and he stares down at it blankly. He'd take a sip if he didn't feel like maybe he'd throw it all back up.

What is *wrong* with him? When did he become this pathetic mooning loser? Better yet, why isn't he doing anything about it?

Someone laughs, too close, and Mike jerks his head up, accidentally catching Wallace's gaze.

And hey, there's the reaction Mike was waiting for, but it doesn't exactly feel as good as he was hoping it would. Wallace's jaw is clenched tight and he looks *furious*. He's definitely pissed that Serge is there, and if Mike had to take a guess, he'd say Wallace caught a glimpse of Cam sharing his flask.

Leoni bares his teeth at him behind Wallace's back, like a rabid dog, and Mike salutes him absently with his paper cup.

Mike's just too damn tired and pissed off at himself to care anymore what Lisa or anyone else thinks.

He slinks out the back of the gym, unbuttons his cuffs

and rolls up his shirtsleeves. He's instantly cold from a biting wind threatening early snow, but it feels good. He fishes a cigarette out of his pack and lights it.

He feels weird. He feels out of place, uncomfortable, and says, "Fuck it," and flicks his cigarette to the ground, kills it with his shiny dress shoe before opening his button-down, tugging it off and balling it up, revealing the worn Lemonheads T-shirt underneath.

Now he's freezing.

It's better than being inside, though. Whatever this is, whatever's going on between him and Wallace now, he doesn't like it.

The metal door behind him makes a creaking noise as it opens. There's a flash of light, and a wall of sound rushes out before abruptly cutting off.

"What the hell is your problem?" Leoni says. He pushes at Mike's chest with the flat of his hand, and Mike stumbles back a step.

"Fuck off, Leoni," Mike says. If he doesn't want to deal with Wallace, he definitely doesn't want to deal with his overgrown lapdog.

Leoni clenches his jaw. He says, "If you don't want," he waves a hand, "*fine. But Serge?*"

"Wait, what?" Mike says. He gets that everyone's a little hot about Mike and his friends *corrupting* Serge, but . . . "What does—"

And Chris Leoni sucker punches him.

Mike blacks out for a second or fifty, and the next thing he knows he's sitting on the sidewalk, legs folded up. His head is fuzzy, brain throbbing.

"Holy shit," Mike says, palming the side of his face. There are pinpricks of light blinking in and out of his vision.

"Fuck," Leoni says.

Mike wants to throw up. "I think—" *I have a concussion,* he tries to say, but it hurts to move his jaw.

"Goddamn it, Tate," Leoni says. He's squatting down in front of Mike. "You're such an asshole. Are you okay?"

"You *punched* me," Mike manages to say. With a sack of rocks, god almighty, it's like Leoni's knuckles are steel plated or brass or something.

"Yeah, well," Leoni says. "You deserved it." He doesn't sound entirely convinced of that fact. *Mike* certainly isn't convinced.

"Fuck," Mike says. He hangs his head between his knees and thinks it's a safe bet he's not going to be able to move for a while. Or do anything that requires his brain to work.

"All right, c'mon, we're going to the hospital."

Mike wants to laugh, but he knows it's a bad idea. "I'm fine."

Leoni makes a scoffing noise and hooks his hands under Mike's arms. "On your feet," he says. "I'm not carrying you."

Mike manages to somehow get his feet under his legs, but he's dizzy, and he leans on Leoni all the way across the parking lot. Leoni's Bronco looms in front of them, and he even lets Leoni open the door for him. He has to practically heft Mike into the seat. Mike's willing to let Leoni do these things for him, considering he broke his face.

Leoni wordlessly gets behind the wheel.

When he starts the car, Mike says, "Shit. Serge." He's pretty sure Omar'll give him a ride home, but he really meant to tell them before he skipped out.

"You're—" Leoni turns to glare at him. At least, Mike thinks that's a glare, his vision's kind of shaky. "You're still worried about Serge?"

"What the *hell*, man." Mike cups his hand over his face, hissing under his breath, "Why the sudden hostility over your best friend's brother? Does Wallace know you hate him?"

"I don't hate Serge," Leoni says, pulling out of the parking lot. "I just don't get why you have to do this to Rook. I don't get *you*."

"Yeah, well." Mike isn't sure he gets himself, either. "That makes two of us."

Mike has to have his face x-rayed, which turns up a hairline fracture across his cheekbone. The nurses fuss over him while he waits for his mom and then they send him home with a prescription for painkillers and an ice pack sometime after midnight.

When he checks his cell, he has one voice mail and four

texts. The voice mail and one of the texts are from Lisa, wondering where the hell he is—he's going to pay for that later, he's sure. Another text is from Omar, letting him know that Wallace left with Serge around ten. The other two are from Meckles. They're pretty funny.

Mike's in way too much pain to fully appreciate them, though—his entire head feels swollen—so he just turns off his phone and goes to bed.

fifteen.

On Monday, the swelling has gone down enough that Mike can actually see out of his left eye. After spending most of Sunday barely being able to even crack his eyelid, he's kind of excited to have a full range of vision again.

He meets Meckles at their lockers and says, "Did you actually text me in the middle of hooking up with Dotty?"

Meckles stares at him. "Did your face get hit by a brick wall?"

Mike flips him off, then slams his locker closed.

Meckles says, "Dude," and reaches out like he wants to touch him, and Mike will not hesitate to break all of Meckles' fingers if they come anywhere near his cheek.

His death glare must properly relay that, because Meckles' arm drops and he just says, "Huh."

"Holy shit," Cam says, coming up behind them. "Holy fucking shit, did you get into a *rumble* Saturday night?"

A rumble would be a lot less embarrassing than admitting he had a disagreement with Leoni's meaty fist. "It's nothing," Mike says.

Cam laughs, throwing an arm over Mike's shoulders as they start off toward homeroom. "No wonder you disappeared. Licking your wounds all day yesterday?"

Mike had pretty much stayed in bed the whole day, under his covers with an ice pack. His mom had coddled him, bringing him ice cream and soda and pizza for dinner. And sometime in between her dropping several heavy hints about Leoni being a gay-bashing homophobe and Mike marathoning *Friends* on Netflix, he realizes that Leoni's mad at him because *Wallace thinks Mike's into his brother.* It's so obvious now, how could he have missed that? Wallace isn't worried that Cam's a bad influence; he's worried that Mike's secretly trying to get into Serge's pants. How fucked up is that?

He doesn't get why they're so quick to assume that he's got the hots for Serge. Serge is a stringy little freshman. He's practically a baby. Sure, maybe he enjoys his company, he's cool to talk to, and he's nice to look at. He's like Wallace, only less of a douche wad. That doesn't mean he *wants* him.

And speaking of the motherfucking ice queen.

There's a bottleneck at the door of their homeroom, and Wallace turns to glare at him. It's weird, seeing Wallace so angry all the time, Mike actually has to fight the urge to try to smooth it all over, tell Wallace, *No, I don't want your baby bro,* because that should be a given. It would be nice if *someone* gave him the benefit of the doubt.

Some of his frigid edges crack when Wallace grimaces at him. "What happened to you?"

"Nothing," Mike says. There's no way he's going to tell Wallace that Leoni punched him. And then drove him to the hospital, and waited with him until his mom showed up, because apparently Leoni has a conscience, even if he complained the entire time he was there. Actually, Mike's a little surprised that Wallace doesn't already know all that, this seems like just the kind of thing they'd want to gossip about.

"He got into a rumble," Cam says gleefully.

Wallace's eyes widen in alarm. "Are you okay?"

"I'm *fine*." Mike threads his hands through his hair, exasperated. "Christ, it's just a black eye." You'd think he was attacked by a bear, the way everyone's reacting.

"Who punched you?" Wallace asks.

Mike blinks at him, a little surprised by Wallace's ferocity. He's still reluctant to say anything, though. He figures Wallace will know soon enough, even if Leoni's currently being quiet about it. "Drop it," he says tiredly.

Wallace's jaw tightens. "Someone must have—"

"*Please*, just drop it?" Mike says, pushing past Wallace to get into the classroom.

"Mike."

Mike glances over his shoulder at him. He opens his mouth to snap, *What?* but Wallace actually looks really concerned, and the word gets stuck in his throat.

• • •

Mike is curled up smoking in the second floor bathroom window well. It's cold with the window cracked open, but there's a radiator just under his feet.

"There's a rumor going around that you were attacked by a gang of ninjas."

Mike looks down from his perch at Serge. He has no idea how Serge can joke like that and *still* look like a thundercloud. "Funny," Mike says.

Serge shrugs, hands in his pockets.

Mike stubs his cigarette out on the metal window frame and shoves the butt into an empty Coke can wedged up against the screen. "Sorry about ditching you Saturday."

"Chris says he beat you up."

Great. That probably means Wallace knows that by now, too.

The corners of Serge's mouth are tilted up.

"No offense, kid," Mike says, shaking his head, "but I'm *really* not after your virtue." If Serge knows about the punch, chances are he probably knows about the bi thing, too.

Serge shrugs again. "I know."

"Thank Christ *somebody* does," Mike says, even though that's probably an exaggeration, considering there are only a handful of people who even know he's into dudes now.

It's still annoying as fuck.

He slips off the sill, swiping his hands on his thighs. "So

what are you hiding out in here for?" he asks. Mike knows why *he's* hiding in there. He'd barely made it out of math that morning without spilling everything to Lisa. There's no way he'd have survived lunch.

"Carter," Serge says darkly.

"Carter," Mike says, head cocked. "Chubby sophomore, wears cardigans—*that* Carter?" He can't imagine him bullying much more than a plate of cookies.

Serge's cheeks heat. "Sophie Carter."

"A girl." Mike isn't going to make fun of him, even though that's his first instinct. Girls can be scary.

"Well, uh. The guys mostly leave me alone, since I kicked Marcus in the nuts. And hang out with you."

Mike slumps a hip against the bank of sinks, pleased. It's cool that he can impress the lower classes with his badassery. Apparently girls of all ages are immune, though, that's a little sad. "She pulling your pigtails?"

Serge makes a face. "I'm going to pretend you didn't say that."

"Is Sophie *hot*?" Mike says, smirking. Teasing Serge will never get old.

Serge looks seriously pissy. "It doesn't matter."

"Like hell it doesn't."

"Do you think my brother's hot?" Serge says. He's got both his eyebrows arched and his arms crossed, like he knows exactly how Mike ticks, and what is it about Mike that somehow lets whiny little scamps grow backbones around him?

Granted, Jason's never maimed anybody's junk, that he knows of.

Mike says, "I'm going to pretend you didn't say that," and he curses Serge's tiny, satisfied smile.

"You stupid, stupid boy," Lisa says.

"I didn't do anything," Mike says into his cell. It's preemptive; Mike isn't sure why Lisa's calling him. It's late Tuesday night and he's already in bed, his laptop paused on an episode of *Buffy*.

"I'm pretty sure that's the problem."

It's late and Mike's face hurts, he doesn't need this cryptic shit. "What?"

"Chris Leoni punched you," she says.

Mike grimaces. "How did you find out?" He's been very carefully avoiding Lisa. A wasted effort, clearly, because everybody around him are dirty whores who can't keep their noses out of things that are totally not their business.

"*Larson* told me," Lisa says, like she can't believe she didn't hear it from *Mike* first, "and Larson heard it from Casper, who overheard Leoni telling Rook."

"Great," Mike says. Fucking *fantastic*. He hopes Larson and Casper can keep their mouths shut, but he's not going to hold his breath.

"You know, there's a really simple solution to this," she says.

Mike knows what she's alluding to, and it's in no way *simple*. When he tells her that, though, she just scoffs. *Scoffs*, like him and Wallace being mortal enemies is some kind of joke.

"You're such a drama queen," Lisa says. "Man up, talk to Rook, and maybe Leoni won't break the other half of your face."

"I seriously hate you," Mike says.

Lisa makes an *aren't you adorable* noise, and says, "You'll hate me more if you mess this up," in a vaguely threatening manner, like maybe Mike'll wake up one day with his eyebrows shaved. Mike thinks he'd look stupid without eyebrows.

He sighs loud and heavy, so she can hear how goddamn weary he is of this entire situation. "Fine," he says.

"Fine, what?"

"I'll talk to Wallace." He will, he totally will. He just makes sure not to specify when.

Thanksgiving is Thursday.

Thanksgiving means Cam and Zack and their dad, because the Scott extended family is all the way across the country in California. It means Uncle Louie and Aunt Doreen and Ella and Em, the twins, who are twelve now and probably still in love with Cam—which would be funnier if Cam didn't enjoy the attention so much.

And it means Gramps and Nana.

Gramps is a true American mutt. He likes football and beer and not talking about his feelings. Mike loves this about him.

Mike's grandmother is a retired air force colonel with the posture and punctuality to prove it. She's ice pale, with blond hair shot with silver, and Mike blames her Nordic roots for his own sharp features. She has a smile like a cat, and strong arms, with the strange ability to hug Mike tight and keep him at arm's length all at the same time.

Right now, he wishes his face didn't still look like someone had taken a sledgehammer to it.

Nana corners him in the hall outside his bedroom, grips his chin with cold fingers and clucks her tongue. "Fighting, Michael?" she says. "I expect more out of you."

"Yes, Nana," Mike says dutifully. It never pays to argue with her.

Nana gazes down at him shrewdly. She's just a hair taller than him, but it's still disconcerting. She says, "Your mother tells me you're queer now."

"She did *not*," Mike says, horrified. He slumps back against the wall, palms catching at the slightly textured wallpaper. His knees feel weak.

"She used the term bisexual," she narrows her eyes, "but no grandson of mine is going to be indecisive."

"I don't think that means I'm in—"

"Michael Allan Tate," Nana says.

Mike swallows hard. Maybe he shouldn't be concentrating on terminology now, since his *seventy-five-year-old grandmother* is confronting him about his sexual preferences. He brings a shaky hand up to rub his dry lower lip. "Yes, ma'am?"

She clasps her hands in front of her chest and says, "Are you, or are you not gay?"

Mike does not want to answer that. He absolutely doesn't, but Nana will just stare at him and stare at him with her pale, scary eyes until he eventually gives up, so there's nothing for it. "I am?"

"Are you asking me or telling me?" Nana says sternly.

Mike wants to die. He wants the roof to collapse and kill them all. "Telling," he says in a very small voice.

She nods once, sharply. "Good. Now, who's the boy?"

Boy? He can't decide if this is worse than accidentally coming out to his mom. At least his mom didn't interrogate him about his love life. "Uh. There's no boy."

"Nonsense. You don't decide to be gay without a boy, that's just poor planning."

"It's not like I *decided*—"

"Ostracized and alone," Nana steamrolls right over his words. "I sincerely doubt your mother raised you to be that irresponsible—"

"I'm not *ostracized*, Nana, oh my god."

Nana straightens up; it's hard for her posture to get any more perfect, but she manages it well, she's even *looming*, damn that lousy inch. "Don't interrupt me, Michael," she says. "It's rude."

Mike presses two fingers over his right eye, fighting a headache. He hasn't even had pie yet. This is so unfair. "Sorry," he says.

"You're lying, but I accept your apology anyway." Nana is simultaneously awesome and terrible.

It's not funny, but Mike finds himself fighting off a hysterical giggle. His *life*—is there anyone else in the world that is this ridiculous and pathetic?

Mike's mom yells up the stairs, "Mom, are you harassing Mike?" and relief swells over him so fast he gets a little dizzy, pushing off from the wall.

Nana gives him a look, a we're-not-finished-young-man look, but precedes him down the stairs. Then she ruins everything by sweeping into the living room and saying, "Of course I'm not harassing Michael, Allison. He's just being ridiculously closemouthed about his boyfriend."

Zack chokes on a sip of beer. "You have a *boyfriend*?" he says.

Cam gets hysterical, the bastard, and snorts into his fist.

"Jesus Christ," Mike says, stunned. He's not sure what just fucking happened. He's praying he's having some sort of mental breakdown, like everyone around him is imaginary.

Nana slaps the back of his head. "Language, Michael."

"Are you fucking *kidding* me?" Mike half yells. She just outed him to his *entire family*.

His aunt and uncle are looking at him like he's an alien, the twins are grinning scarily, and Nana's mouth goes small and pinched. Mike would care if he didn't *hate* her. Nana is dead to him. He's going to pay for it later, but right now he just wants to stomp off in a hissy fit, slam his bedroom door, and sulk until Christmas.

"Michael," Mom says. It's her disappointed voice. Mike doesn't think he's warranted that. *He* hasn't done anything wrong.

He sullenly flops down on the couch next to Cam, crossing his arms over his chest. Cam punches him in the shoulder, mouth stretched into this huge mocking smile, the bitch.

Mom gives him an arched eyebrow before shuffling Aunt Doreen and Nana into the kitchen. On any other mom that would probably mean he's headed for a grounding, but Mike's never been grounded in his whole life, not even for the time he and Cam accidentally set the garage on fire.

Gramps dials up the volume on the TV so the Eagles game drowns out whatever the twins are giggling about.

"So," Zack says, rolling his beer bottle between his palms. He draws the word out, waggling his eyebrows in a leer, reminding Mike that, yes, no matter how cool Mike thinks Zack is, he's still related to Cam. "You're gay."

Mike's heart is thudding so hard his arms feel numb, but he scowls over at Zack and flips him off.

• • •

The day after Thanksgiving, snow-pocalypse happens. It starts in the early hours, and when Mike finally rolls out of bed around noon, the world is layered with at least a foot of pure white powder. It's still snowing heavily, and doesn't look ready to let up anytime soon.

Rosie is ecstatic.

Mike still wants the world to fuck off and die, but he's no match for Rosie's enthusiasm. He pulls on three layers of sweatpants, two hoodies, and shoves wool-covered feet into his snow boots. He tugs his knit cap down over his ears and gets out an old pair of snow gloves, the navy Batman ones, before following Rosie out into the front yard.

It's quiet out. The snow is falling so thick and swift that there aren't any cars on the road, so the only sounds are the hushed pings of snowflakes on snowflakes.

And then there's a loud whoop, echoing down the street from the Wallace house, and Teeny and Lilith are racing toward them, a dark blob of Serge wandering along behind.

Mike doesn't ask where Wallace is. Instead, he lets himself be drawn into a snowball fight, girls against guys, and he and Serge make a fort in the middle of Mike's lawn, high and thick walled. They take too much time building the fort instead of stocking up on snowballs, and Teeny and Rosie are sneaky little shits and start pelting them rapid-fire. Mike and Serge lose spectacularly, but it makes Rosie happy, so Mike doesn't honestly care.

Their neighborhood is completely flat. A tragedy for sledding, but in this weather they definitely aren't driving down to Pindel Elementary, the closest hill worth any effort. They'd have to wait for the snow to stop and then for the plows to come through before attempting that. Which means the girls expend most of their energies making a snow house, two snow dogs, and a snow cow before Mrs. Wallace calls them inside for hot chocolate.

Serge stays out with Mike. He's frowning down at their fort, like he doesn't quite like how it turned out.

"So, uh." Mike rubs his gloves together and watches Serge kick at the sides of it. "Where's your brother?" He totally wasn't going to ask about Wallace, he doesn't know why he always does this to himself.

Serge rolls his eyes and kicks harder at the wall of snow.

They put a lot of work into that, though, even if it's kind of lopsided, so Mike pushes him aside and hunches down to smooth out the hole he made.

Serge takes the opportunity to shove snow down the back of his sweatshirt.

"Son of a bitch!" Mike yelps, jerking to his feet and shivering, trying to shake the snow out.

Serge laughs and backs away, hands up. "C'mon, it was an accident," he says. Mike scoops up some snow, pats it together as he slowly advances on Serge. He's trying to be menacing, but by the way Serge is grinning at him, he doesn't think it works.

Serge matches his steps, moving backward, and Mike lunges for him. He grabs at the pockets of his pants and manages to get the snowball up under the front of Serge's jacket.

Serge dances away with a shout. "You *suck*."

"You started this," Mike says, and then dodges another attack. He stomps right through their fort by accident, trips over a downed tree branch, and then gets tackled into the snow cow, face-first.

It only takes a few minutes of all-out war—which Mike is *definitely* winning—for Serge to shake snow off his gloves, say, "Fuck this," and "Later," and leave for his house, getting in out of the cold.

Mike shouts, "Pussy!" after him and sprawls out on his back in the pathetic remains of their fort. He stares up at the gray sky and blinks snow out of his eyes. Flakes, fatter and slower than before, stick to his eyelashes, and melt down his temples to freeze again in his hair. He rubs the wet palms of his snow gloves over his cheeks and thinks about following Serge's example and heading inside. He's fucking soaked.

"You're kind of a jerk."

Mike tilts his head back a little to see Wallace standing above him. He's only got jeans and a sweater on. "Yeah?" Mike says.

Wallace stares down at him, face ruddy but mainly unreadable, the lines of his brows and mouth flat. Finally,

Wallace heaves a sigh. "Why do you have to be so difficult?" he says.

Mike shrugs, shoulders pressing into the snow. "Sorry."

"You're really not," Wallace says, and then he hunches down, fists both his hands in the front of Mike's hoodie, and yanks him to his feet.

Mike's unsteady, so he grabs for Wallace's forearms. He suddenly finds himself entirely too close to Wallace's face.

"You're really fucking annoying," Wallace says, but he sounds kind of breathless and his eyes have gone navy. "And Serge says you've got a—frankly disturbing obsession with alternative rock."

That's not Mike's fault. It's just that he hero-worshipped Zack Scott from a very young, impressionable age. At least he's not obsessed with power pop or, god forbid, *country*. In the grand scheme of things, alternative rock is *awesome*.

Mike isn't going to get into that now, though.

Mike shifts his grip to Wallace's wrists. He's close enough to Wallace to smell the mint on his breath, and something in Mike's chest seizes up, serious as a heart attack. The world is muffled around him, both from the roaring of nerves in his ears and the heavy, blanketing snow. "Are you sure this isn't an 'I'm gay, you're gay, let's be gay together' kind of thing?" Mike says softly. He hadn't been planning on saying that. Hell, he's not even sure where it came from, but now that he thinks about it, it's totally a valid point.

Wallace frowns. "Actually, it's more of an 'I'm gay, I've

been pining for you since I hit puberty and realized what dicks are for' kind of thing," he says. His hands twist tighter in Mike's sweatshirt, even though Mike hasn't moved an inch either way. "This is kind of an unexpected bonus."

Mike stares at the flush that's slowly creeping up and over Wallace's cheeks. His heart kick-starts into something resembling a regular rhythm again, amusement a slow bloom deep inside. "Pining?"

Wallace shifts awkwardly on his feet. "Uh."

"Really?" *Pining* makes Wallace sound like a big, teary-eyed girl. Mike wants to laugh, but he feels like it's a really inappropriate time. Or it feels like a great time to Mike, something to slice the insane tenseness hanging over them, except he thinks Wallace would take it the entirely wrong way.

Wallace says, "The pining part still really sucks, by the way. You don't . . . ?" He makes a face. "Not even a little bit?"

Mike's brow wrinkles. "What?"

"Like me?"

Honestly? Right now Mike feels like he's stuck in one of Rosie's Disney channel shows. He cocks his head, biting his bottom lip. Finally, he says, "*Like* you, like you?"

"Oh, fuck off," Wallace says, but he's smiling a little.

Mike drops his hands from Wallace's arms and says, "I can't believe you thought I wanted to bone your *brother*." He'd honest-to-god thought Wallace had been mad that they were corrupting him.

"So . . . is that a no?" Wallace says, finally releasing Mike's sweatshirt.

It takes a couple seconds for Mike to realize Wallace is still waiting for an answer—does Mike *like* him?

"It's not a no," Mike says. Then, after a pause, "I don't know what you want me to say."

"Fuck, Mike." Wallace laughs, choked, like it's not actually funny. "You realize I've totally put myself out there for you. A couple times, now. How the hell can you not know what I want you to say?"

It's different, Mike thinks, than it was with J. J. With J. J., he *knew* he didn't like him. He liked certain parts of J. J., but not enough to make up a whole that wasn't a complete smug and pretentious asswipe. With Wallace, all his dislikes have apparently been based on a false premise. There's still a tiny niggling of doubt, though, so Mike asks, "Are you sure you're not just fucking with me?" just to be sure.

Wallace growls under his breath, and Mike feels it all the way down to his toes.

He doesn't know what makes him do it. Maybe it's the way Wallace's eyes narrow in frustration, shoulders tense, like he's one second away from stomping his foot in a temper tantrum. Maybe it's the way Wallace's fingers clench, like he's fighting the urge to reach out and grab. Maybe it's because Wallace made all the moves last time, he's said all the right words, and all Mike's done is throw it all back into his face.

197

Mike slowly lifts his hand, bites the tip of his middle finger and tugs off his glove, lets it drop to the ground between their feet. He does the same with the other, then he reaches out, spreads warm fingers on Wallace's cold throat. Wallace shivers, and there's that curve of his mouth, the smirk Mike's actually *missed*, and Mike thinks Wallace is tense now for an entirely different reason.

"What are you doing?" Wallace asks, voice rough.

Mike says, "I have no fucking clue," as he guides Wallace's face toward his.

Wallace is taller than him. Mike isn't thrilled about that, but Wallace ducks his head down and meets him halfway. It's nothing like before, when Mike had been burning alcohol and Wallace had been, Mike thinks now, full of forceful mock-confidence. There's a softness to his mouth, now, Wallace's jaw relaxed under his palms.

"Mike," Wallace says, just a tiny, irritating millimeter from Mike. "Mike, are you—"

"Stop talking," Mike says.

Their lips are dry with cold, chapped, catching roughly at the slight tilt, mouth to mouth. Mike hangs there for a moment and breathes hotly in a false kiss. A split second of absolute panic zips down his spine, before freezing cold hands come up to grip the back of his neck, tugging him so he falls along the length of Wallace's body. Mike's eyes are closed by the time Wallace takes over and starts kissing him for real.

Mike makes a small sound into his mouth, hands scrabbling with fabric, then gripping tightly at the collar of Wallace's sweater. He arches into Wallace, has to go up on his tiptoes, making the slant of mouths aggressive.

Wallace tastes like toothpaste, like premeditation. Mike would be annoyed by that if Wallace's teeth didn't scrape over Mike's bottom lip, if he didn't let up just enough to pant and murmur, "Fuck." Mike can barely stand it.

Mike moves his hands down to press under Wallace's sweater, palming the small of his back, and Wallace shivers.

There's a broken laugh and Wallace says, "Shit, I should've worn a coat," and Mike grins, moving his lips, damp now, across Wallace's jaw.

"You should probably go back inside," Mike says with a groan.

"Yeah," Wallace says, shoving a hand through his hair, disturbing fat, fluffy flakes that haven't fully dissolved yet. They fall on Mike's cheeks and he thumps his forehead onto Wallace's shoulder.

Everything's wet with half-melted snow. Mike's fingers feel raw. He flexes the joints, pressing the pads into Wallace's bare skin before he finally lets go and takes a small step back.

The snow has nearly slowed to a stop, but everything's gray with twilight.

"Do you want to—" Wallace cuts himself off, tips his head back. "Never mind."

"What? Do I want to what?" Mike says, more eager than he intends to.

Wallace shakes his head, but he smiles a little and says, "Do you want to go see a movie or something? Next week, maybe?"

Mike wants to say no, just because he's not used to saying yes. Yes to whatever this is. Instead, for the first time, he says, "Sure," and hopes it's not a mistake.

sixteen.

By Monday, most of the town has dug them-selves out of the eighteen inches of snow that had fallen over the course of Black Friday.

There's a nauseating mixture of nervousness and giddy anticipation roiling around Mike's stomach. He's having trouble figuring out how he's supposed to act around Wallace now. Is he supposed to be nice to him? Are they supposed to, like, talk to each other? It's *weird*.

"What's up with you?" Lisa asks him in math.

"I'm having a small mental breakdown," Mike says absently, staring down at his notebook. He's wondering whether he has to switch seats with Leoni in English and doodling cats in the corners of his vector diagram. He doesn't *want* to switch seats. He wants to sit next to Mo and make fun of Beckett—god, they *hate* Beckett; only pretentious weirdos like Beckett. Mike and Mo agree that existentialism is for pussies.

Lisa pokes him with her pencil. "About what?"

Mike looks up and blinks at her. "What?"

"You're having a breakdown?" Lisa says.

"I said that out loud?" Mike rubs a hand over his mouth. He feels like a zombie, like he hasn't slept in three days. He also feels—he's not sure, but he thinks he's actually *looking forward* to going out with Wallace. He kind of wants to smile stupidly at Lisa and gossip about making out with Wallace in the snow. He obviously has brain damage from the cold.

"You're spacey today. Why are you so spacey?" Lisa asks. "You're not high, are you?"

Mike frowns. "No." That would probably solve a lot of his problems, though.

"Okay," Lisa says, in a way that implies it's not okay. She totally doesn't believe him, but she's going to let it slide, just this once. It involves narrowed eyes and calculated tapping of her pencil.

Mike is saved by the teacher, and he pretends to pay attention for once, until the bell rings and he can slip off to English before Lisa can force him into a deeper conversation.

Of course, he gets to English and remembers why he probably should've hidden out in the second floor boys' bathroom instead.

Wallace is already in his seat, pulling out *Waiting For Godot*, and he glances up at Mike with a truly ridiculous-looking grin. Mike stops short at the open door, staring, stomach doing this horrible nervous fluttering thing, until Vin Yoon shoulders him out of the way with a dirty look. Fucking *Vin*. Mike scowls at him, and when he turns back toward Wallace, Leoni is taking his regular seat next to him. The fluttering doesn't exactly go away, but something in all his limbs relaxes.

He makes his way back to Mo and her rant on *Endgame*, and it's—thank Christ—like any other crappy day of the week.

For the most part, Mike's week goes exactly the same as usual. Except with a marked lack of glaring in Wallace's direction, an occasional nod of hello, and that single, semi-awkward moment Wednesday morning, when Wallace had cornered him at his locker just before homeroom and officially asked him out for Friday night.

Mike would like to say he hadn't blushed all over his fair-skinned body, but that would be a huge lie. Wallace had loomed all up in his space, confidence back in spades, and Mike had stammered out a yes like a virginal schoolgirl.

On Thursday, Dotty says, "You and Rook kiss and make up?" and Mike chokes on spit and nothing and almost coughs up a lung.

Dotty pats his back so hard Mike nearly stumbles. "Geez," she says. "Are you okay?"

"Fine," Mike gasps. And then he has a holy-shit epiphany—Mike realizes he's going to have to *tell people*. Not just Lisa or Jay or his crazy grandmother. This probably isn't going to stay a secret, judging by the extreme lack of discretion Wallace has shown so far.

The thing is, it may not *seem* like a big deal—Mike's been accidentally outed to so many people these past couple months, he should be used to it—but it totally is. Once everyone knows, there's no going back. There's no changing his mind, no brushing it off.

Except Wallace isn't exactly out and proud to the masses yet, either, so . . . maybe Wallace *wants* this to be a secret? Maybe he won't want anyone knowing that he's dating Mike at all.

Mike isn't sure which scenario is worse and he suddenly feels like throwing up all over Dotty's shoes. He doesn't, but it's a close thing.

"You look weird," Dotty says.

"Thanks," Mike says dryly, and Dotty grins.

"Seriously, you're acting weird, too," she says.

Mike shrugs tightly. At some point, he might tell her. Or maybe she'll just find out, which is way more likely, and it's going to be weird if and when that happens, but he's not going to do anything about that *now*.

Right now, he's going to go to his Spanish class and fake his way through *Don Quixote*.

After school on Friday, Mike fidgets through dinner with Rosie and his mom and then locks himself in his room and panics.

Mike has no idea what he's supposed to do on a date with

a guy. Logically, he knows it can't be much different than any other kind of date, but *illogically*—illogically, Mike is freaking out.

This is the only possible explanation for why he calls Scalzetti.

"Michael," J. J. says when he picks up. "Hello."

"Hey," Mike says.

There's a pointed silence. Then J. J. says, "And you called me, why?"

Mike takes a deep breath. He says, "I have a date."

"Good for you," J. J. says coolly. "I fail to see how this is relevant to me."

"I have a date with a *guy*," Mike says.

"That actually makes it worse, Michael. You *can* see that, right?"

"Um." It's possible Mike didn't think this through.

J. J. sighs noisily. "You're freaking out."

"Uh, *yeah*." Mike thinks that's pretty obvious.

"I'm not your gay love guru," J. J. says, only he sounds more resigned than pissy. "What's the problem?"

Mike opens and closes his mouth dumbly, presses his lips together. He's not sure he can explain it. They've already kissed; going out should be the easy part, right? "I don't know," he finally says.

"Well," J. J. says, "who are you going out *with*?"

Mike grimaces to himself, but it's not like it matters if J. J. knows. "Rook Wallace."

"*Rook?* You know," J. J. says, tone lighter, "I think I can forgive you for passing me over if you had that panting after you. How on earth did you manage to land *him?*"

"Fuck if I know," Mike says.

J. J. *hmmm*s thoughtfully. He says, "Well, I'm not sure what you want from me, but I'd advise you not to screw this up."

"Thanks," Mike says. Everyone around him is so goddamn *helpful*, right?

"I'm serious," J. J. says. "Rook's dreamy and tall and way too good for you. You'll probably have to bathe regularly now. I know it's a hardship, but you'll have to at least *try* to be hygienic. Lord knows why *I* find you attractive, Michael, when you generally smell like weed and broken hobo dreams, but I'll give you five gold stars for your kissing technique."

Mike chokes on a laugh. "Right."

"Your mouth is very important, Michael," J. J. says, completely serious, and his voice goes a little husky, which definitely should *not* spark off something in Mike's belly, but it's not like he can help it.

Mike's mouth is suddenly dry, but he manages a thick "Yeah."

J. J. inhales sharply. "Oh, don't tease me. I know you won't put out."

Mike doesn't actually know who's teasing who here, so he figures it's a good time to hang up. There's just something about Scalzetti. Mike almost wishes he *could* stand the guy—they'd probably have some fun together. He says, "I gotta go."

"Of course," J. J. says. He adds, "Just relax and have fun. Don't do anything I wouldn't do."

It's not really the kind of advice Mike had been hoping for. He's got the feeling that there's not a whole lot J. J. wouldn't do. He says, "Thanks," anyway.

Mike showers, because he does *shower*, thanks very much, *J. J.*

He uses actual shampoo on his hair and jerks off thinking about Wallace's hands and J. J.'s mouth, because he's messed up in the head, and then he enters this strange realm of calm as he gets dressed. This is going to go fine, he tells himself. It's just a movie, and then maybe they'll make out in the backseat of Wallace's car.

He changes twice, because Rosie looks at him weird when he puts on a button-down, and he ends up in a newish T-shirt and jeans. He looks pretty much like he always does and he figures that's not a bad thing.

Mom is sitting in the kitchen with an entire apple pie when he wanders in, fiddling with the hem of his shirt. She tries and fails to look like she didn't just shove an enormous forkful into her mouth and stares him down with an arched eyebrow.

"What?" he says.

She waves her fork around. "Nothing," she says thickly, cheeks puffed out like a chipmunk.

"Right." He doesn't expect anything, it's not like he *told* her about the date. As far as she's concerned, he could be doing anything he regularly does on a Friday. Meeting up with Cam and Meckles. Playing drunken flashlight tag in the woods. Setting some garbage on fire. Hiding from the cops. The usual.

Still, there's a particular way she says, "Be safe," like she's not talking about tying a scooter to the back of Omar's van and heading for the highway, but Mike's not going to call her on it—that's a conversation he's going to avoid as long as possible.

At seven o'clock, he shrugs on his army jacket and meets Wallace at the end of his driveway. He pops open the passenger door and slides in; the heater's on high, blasting air and noise, and the radio's on low—some hip-hop station. Mike can feel the bass through his seat.

Mike slams the door shut, and when the dome light winks out, Wallace leans over and kisses him—shallow and so quick Mike's a little breathless when Wallace pulls away. And then he follows him, knee wedged into the center console, hands gripping Wallace's jacket, because that wasn't nearly enough of a hello—this is what his pants are telling him. After a thorough mapping of Wallace's mouth, Mike sits back in the seat and says, "Hey."

"Christ," Wallace breathes.

"You started it," Mike says. He's a little smug. He doesn't know why he was so worried; Mike is actually *fantastic* at this dating guys thing.

Wallace chuffs a laugh. "Yeah, um. I pretty much wanted to do that all week."

"Cool." Mike slumps down so his knees are hitting the dash.

Wallace flashes him a look before putting the car in gear. Mike can't quite tell what his expression is in the dim light, but he's betting on surprise. He's probably been waiting for Mike to freak out. Never mind the fact that Mike actually *did* freak out—it was hours ago, so it totally doesn't count.

When Wallace pulls into the parking lot for the local AMC, Mike feels more relieved than he'd ever admit aloud. The AMC is smaller than the Franklin and closer to their houses, so they're less likely to run into anyone they know there who's below the age of forty. It's not like he would have *minded* seeing people he knows, two guys going to the movies doesn't automatically scream *date*, but considering Mike would tell anyone who'd listen that Wallace was his evil archnemesis, born from the unholy union of Lucifer and a goat, it'd be a little weird seeing them in public together. It would require *explanations*.

Mike has a brief, tiny panic attack when they buy tickets—is he supposed to buy? Are they going Dutch?— but it turns out to not be a big deal. Wallace steps up to the booth first, pays without asking Mike, and Mike's actually

209

okay with that. He stuffs his hands into his pockets and slouches next to Wallace.

Wallace hands him his ticket and Mike cocks his head toward the snack bar. "Candy?" he says.

"Sure, but you better be buying," Wallace says.

Mike grins, and the rest is surprisingly easy.

Mike loses track of what's happening on-screen twenty minutes in, when Wallace's legs spread and their knees touch and Mike goes instantly hard, because apparently his earlier orgasm did nothing to calm his libido. It figures.

Mike shifts in his seat, sinks farther down and presses his knee back. If it wasn't a family theater, he'd push up the armrest in between them and try for the whole thigh. He feels Wallace's eyes on the side of his face, brief and intense. He's not ignoring him, exactly, just concentrating on the heat spreading out from where their legs are touching. By the time he remembers that there's a movie playing, he's totally lost the narrative.

He doesn't particularly care, but he also doesn't feel like sitting through another two hours of this.

He leans into Wallace, elbow on the rest, leveraging him up so his mouth is close to Wallace's ear. He says, "You watching this?"

"I'm—" Wallace turns to look at him, their noses nearly touching. "Yes."

Mike narrows his eyes, nods. "Right."

Wallace faces the screen again, the corner of his mouth tight. His hands are curled into fists on his thighs, and Mike watches him shift and squirm, and thinks, *Well, well*. Never let it be said that Mike is *shy*.

He stays angled toward Wallace, oh-so-casually drapes his arm over the armrest. Wallace tenses when Mike's fingers slide under his forearm to lay his palm flat against Wallace's jeans.

Mike stifles a grin. "Sure?"

"Yes," Wallace says, though it's more a hiss than a word.

Mike wants to laugh. The tips of his fingers scrape Wallace's inseam and Wallace jerks away from him and gets to his feet in one continuous motion, grabbing Mike's arm. For a split second Mike thinks he's going to yell at him, that Wallace is pissed off, but he only pulls Mike up and pushes him out toward the center aisle instead.

Mike trips over his feet and an elderly couple at the end of the row, swallowing down a laugh and murmuring, "Sorry."

He feels like a little kid, stomping down the stadium stairs and swinging around to the doors, amusement bubbling up his throat. They don't even make it out of the dark hallway before Wallace pushes Mike up against the wall, curves his palms over Mike's ass and hauls his hips up to slot into his.

Mike has to muffle a yelp into Wallace's shoulder.

"You're such a jerk," Wallace says, a raspy whisper.

"Shhhh," Mike says, shaking a little with suppressed laughter. He can't believe they're doing this. He can feel Wallace hard against the crease of his hip, and Mike's mind's eye briefly flashes back to gay porn and scary dicks, but instead of fear and disgust, he just wants to get closer, maybe, definitely with more bare skin involved. It turns out he just needed a little context.

Mike's so fucking turned on, and he thinks any more friction and he'll come in his pants, right there.

He presses his open mouth into Wallace's throat, hooks an ankle around Wallace's calf, the other foot straining on its tiptoes.

Wallace says, "This is a bad idea."

He's right. The ushers are probably going to find them any second now. Mike tugs on the back of Wallace's shirt. "Car," Mike says. He'd even settle for the bathroom. He's not picky.

The lobby isn't very crowded, and Wallace pulls him along with a hand on his wrist, and Mike hides his mouth with his other hand, because he can't stop laughing. It's like he's high, only really it's just nerves and excitement and the fact that he's going to get laid. Hopefully. If they don't get arrested first.

Wallace has to unlock the car door manually, which is such a pain in the ass. Mike drapes himself along Wallace's back, though, and hooks his fingers into the waistband of Wallace's jeans, waiting for him to lever the front seat forward, and then he's being twisted around and shoved backward into the cramped backseat of the two-door Chevy.

"Do you always put out on the first date?" Wallace asks.

"Hell, yeah," Mike says, scooting farther into the car as Wallace crawls in, one knee between Mike's spread legs. He's a *guy*. He's sixteen. Christ, he's probably not going to last very long.

Wallace grins, the dome light casting a shadow over his eyes, and it's his wolf grin—one that makes him look like he wants to take Mike apart with his teeth. Mike's all for that grin right now.

"Shut the door," Mike says. They're *totally* going to get arrested.

When Wallace finally kisses him, he tastes like Runts, like sugar, but Mike is too on edge to savor the sweetness. He sucks in a breath when Wallace gropes for the button on his jeans, skimming warm fingers on his belly. At the sound of his zipper, Mike's breathing grows louder, ragged, and he suddenly wishes they'd turned the car on, that they had the buzz of the radio to drown them out.

"Okay?" Wallace says.

Mike nods. "Yeah." And then Wallace's hand snakes into his boxers. "Fuck, yeah," his voice breaks.

Wallace chuckles against his cheek, which,—*fuck* that. His turn. Mike arches his back, grabs hold of Wallace's shoulders and turns his head, just enough to bite into Wallace's mouth. When Wallace's grip on him stutters, Mike worms his hand down the front of Wallace's jeans, and Wallace makes a gratifying squeaky noise.

Mike gets Wallace's pants all the way open just about the time Wallace's breath has fallen back into a rhythm, and the heavy, hot feel of him in Mike's hand—embarrassingly enough—is what sets him off. The rush up from his toes, through his balls, is almost a surprise, and Mike worries he squeezes too hard in that instant, heart caught in his throat.

But if it bothers Wallace, he doesn't say, following Mike short seconds later.

"Shit," Mike breathes. He pushes Wallace's shoulders back until he's flat against the seat and Mike is flush against him.

"That was too fast," Wallace says with a sigh. Mike tenses, but Wallace quickly clarifies. "Like, *over* too fast."

Mike totally agrees. He's still breathing hard, but he already wants to do it again. Maybe not in a car, though. Sex in a car actually kind of sucks balls. Wallace's legs are all over the place, and Mike doesn't know where to put his arms. He feels really fucking great anyway. And they'll have other chances, elsewhere. Lots of them.

Mike's sweat is cooling quickly without the heat on, and

he shivers a little, tucks his head into Wallace's neck for warmth. Mike's ass is hanging off the edge of the seat, and Wallace's hand on his hip and his long leg thrown over Mike's thigh are pretty much the only things keeping him in place. Doesn't matter, though—it's enough.

It's pretty awkward, untangling themselves, wiping off with a bunch of McDonald's napkins from the foot well, and migrating to the front seats. Wallace keeps elbowing him, and Mike accidentally kicks him a couple times in the thigh. Mike's shirt is more than a little gross, too. He feels weird and sticky, sitting in the passenger seat.

Wallace turns on the car, and there's a blast of clammy air from the heater before he dials it down a few notches. "So," he says.

The digital clock on the radio says it's only eight thirty.

"Yeah," Mike says with an exhale.

"I was planning on maybe getting ice cream after the movie," Wallace says.

Mike could go for some ice cream. There's really never a time Mike *couldn't* go for ice cream. He rubs his palms on his thighs and says, "Okay, sure." Somehow this, right then, is so much more uncomfortable than cuddling in the backseat. It's like his brain shuts down when they're touching, and now that he can think again it's just really strange, knowing that he's touched Wallace's dick.

He thinks maybe Wallace is experiencing the same thing.

There's a Dairy Queen five miles outside of Morrison. They're quiet on the drive, silence thickening around them until Mike can't think of anything to say that won't be unbelievably lame.

The Dairy Queen is crowded. Mike tries not to panic. He just has to take a deep breath and dive in.

Mike recognizes a couple kids from different grades, but none of their *friends* are there, at least. There isn't even anyone in their class there. Small mercies.

They wait in line and Mike slouches next to Wallace and Wallace jitters his leg until they both have ice cream—an Oreo Cookies Blizzard for Wallace and a Reese's Peanut Butter Cup Blizzard for Mike—and then they sit across from each other in a hard plastic red-and-white booth.

Mike bows his head and stabs his Blizzard with his spoon.

Wallace kicks out with a foot, knocking it against Mike's sneaker, then grins at him when Mike glances up.

"Hey," Wallace says.

Half of Mike's mouth quirks up. "What?"

Wallace shakes his head, still grinning. "Nothing."

Mike rolls his eyes. "You're secretly a big dork, right?"

"I didn't think it was a secret," Wallace says. He nudges his cup toward Mike. "Want some?"

Mike dips his spoon in, at the same time gesturing at his own ice cream, and somehow they end up switching cups and talking about Meckles, and how hilarious he is with Dotty, and then Wallace wrinkles his nose and says, "You and Serge. I didn't like that."

"Oh my god, Wallace, I'm his *friend*," Mike says. "I saved him from getting beat up by assholes! I don't see how that's a bad thing."

"You can call me Rook, you know," Wallace says.

"*Wallace*," Mike says, because Rook just sounds weird, even in his head, "you don't honestly want me to stop hanging out with your brother, do you?"

Wallace shrugs, but he looks reluctant. "I guess not."

"You guess—" Mike cuts himself off with an amused snort. Wallace is jealous, and Mike's trying not to find that completely hysterical. "Serge is a weirdo, but I like him." And speaking of that. "Actually, your whole family's strange," he says. "Doesn't your mom collect clowns?"

Wallace arches an eyebrow. "I've been introduced to Sandwich. And, uh. Box Head?"

Mike nods. His family is weird, too. "I see your point. But Lilith is—"

"Cripplingly shy," Wallace says.

"Let me guess," Mike says, grinning. "Teeny takes after you."

"Teeny wants to be Miss Teen USA."

"Right," Mike laughs. "*Totally* takes after you."

Wallace's mouth curves into that smirk again and his eyes are amused. He says, "My dad's normal."

"There is no normal, Wallace," Mike says, thinking of what Lisa said. He taps his spoon on the chipped Formica table. "We're all fucked up."

Wallace cocks his head, quizzical. "You really think that?"

"I don't know. Kind of." He's starting to believe, though, that being fucked up has its benefits.

Wallace doesn't walk him to his door, but he does lean across the console and kiss him. It seems weird, at first, even though they've been kissing all night. He holds his hands up, fingers spread, feeling ridiculous, and then clutches the front of Wallace's coat and kisses him back.

"Uh. This was fun," Wallace says when he pulls away, barely.

"Yeah, it—"

Wallace tugs their faces close again, palming Mike's neck. He nips at Mike's lower lip and rests his thumb under Mike's chin, moving back again. "Three weeks. I have tickets to see Evan Dando—"

"Evan Dando?" Mike says. "Lead singer of the Lemonheads Evan Dando?"

"Yeah." Wallace nods, a smug little knowing smile on his lips that Mike kind of wants to bite off him, except *Evan Dando*! "He's playing an acoustic Christmas set in Philadelphia."

"I *know*," Mike says. "That's three hours away. On Christmas Eve."

"I know. Look, you don't have to. I just thought, because you liked them, maybe you'd—" Wallace shrugs.

Mike punches him on the shoulder. "Shut the fuck up, Wallace, of *course* I want to go." He just has to weasel out of going to his grandparents', which should be fun. Nana'll probably be okay with it if he mentions having a *boy*. A boy something. Not a boyfriend, obviously, but someone worth being gay with. Nana will approve of that, because she's a crazy person.

"Good," Wallace says.

Mike nods. "Yeah." He gets a little lost, staring at Wallace, and then he remembers they're still sitting in his driveway and that he should probably get out of the car. "Thanks," he says. "For the movie."

Wallace arches his eyebrow, silently mocking. "The best movie."

There's an expanding ball of warmth in Mike's chest. He clears his throat and reaches for the door handle. "See you," he says.

Wallace nods. "Yeah, bye."

Mike doesn't mean to do it, but he ends up spending half the night lying in bed, staring at his ceiling. He doesn't feel antsy or anxious, only like he's riding on some mellow high. It's a little like how he felt when he first started dating Lisa—back when they actually *were* dating, not just twistedly saving each other from boredom. Back when it was new and exciting and Mike wasn't sure where it was going, but it didn't matter, because right at that moment it was *amazing*.

It's a little like that, but not quite.

He still feels nervous as hell, like this could end up being a huge motherfucking disaster. One that could hurt a lot more than just deciding they, him and Wallace, don't work together, after all.

But, fuck, it's even *more* exciting than with Lisa. Mike is a giant tool; it's nearly three in the morning, and he's *still* smiling giddily up at nothing. There's a tingling in the tips of his fingers and toes and it feels so good that he's just shy of jerking off again. He squirms a little against his sheets, and then he thinks, *fuck it*, and slips a hand down his stomach and into his shorts.

seventeen.

"You're in a good mood," Omar says. He's
perched on the edge of the pool table in Meckles' basement,
feet resting on the arm of the couch across from it.

Mike bobs his head. "I guess." He's in a *great* mood. He
feels like grinning at everybody. He bows his head to his
guitar, face hot, and strums an absent chord. Goddamn it,
he's acting like a dumbass, but he can't help himself.

"What's up with you?" Meckles asks.

Mike shrugs and says, "So, I'm, uh, sort of dating Wallace. Well, *a* date. I had a date with Wallace last night." He
didn't *plan* this, but his brain obviously thought it was a
good time to talk, with all of them hanging out at Meckles',
halfheartedly jamming. He kind of wants to stuff the words
back into his mouth as soon as he's said them. Omar has a
deer-in-headlights look on his face and Mike's heart jumps
up into his throat.

"Isn't Lilith eleven?" Meckles asks, confused.

A second later Cam sits up from his sprawl on the couch
and says, "Wait, *Rook*? Don't you hate him?"

Mike dips his head. He palms the back of his neck; it's damp with sweat and nerves. He says, "I don't *hate* him."

He takes in Meckles' absolutely fucking baffled expression, and goes on. "Apparently"—he takes a deep breath—"I like guys."

There. It's done. It's out there, spelled out and highlighted for all of them now. He feels a little like all the air's been sucked from the room, but also like a giant weight has lifted off his chest. Throwing up has not been taken completely off the table, though.

Meckles says, "You're *gay*?" He looks pale and stricken, and a little horrified. He looks how Mike had felt, at the beginning of this mess, so Mike understands.

That doesn't mean it doesn't still hurt, though.

"Technically," Mike says, a little shakily, "I'm bi."

And then Omar—Mike's fucking *rock*—whips off his bass and silently stalks from the room.

Omar doesn't pick him up for school on Monday.

Mike waits at the front window for fifteen minutes before giving in and waking up his mom for a ride and a late note. She gives him sympathetic, worried glances on the way. When they pull up in front of the school, she puts the car in park and shifts in her seat to look at him fully.

"You know, I let the black eye slide, even though you ended up at the *hospital*," she says pointedly.

Mike picks at the strap of his bag. "Yeah." He *really* doesn't want to talk about this.

She sighs. "Just . . . are you okay?"

"I'm—" He stares out the windshield. Two girls hurry past, books hugged to their chests. One of them waves back at the pickup truck idling at the curb in front of Mom's car before disappearing inside. "I don't know," he says.

"All right," she says. She reaches over and squeezes his wrist. "If you ever want to talk . . ."

"That's okay," Mike says. His mom is great, he loves her a lot, but he absolutely does not want to talk to her about how much liking dudes is apparently fucking up his friendships.

"I mean it." She shakes his arm. She looks grimly determined, like she'd take on the world for him if she could, if he'd let her, and Mike's reminded of all the ways she tells Rosie's teachers to shove it up their asses whenever they call Rosie *special*. How she routinely got thrown out of his Little League games for yelling at the umps and coaches, and sometimes the snack stand volunteers when they ran out of hot dogs. How she always let Cam sleep over after his mom died, even if it meant dealing with two hopped up seven-year-olds watching R-rated action movies at eleven on a school night.

Mike doesn't even want to think about what she'd do to Omar if she knew, but it's kind of reassuring to remember she has his back, anyhow.

He says, "Thanks, Mom," and manages a shaky smile.

The next day, he gets up twenty minutes early and bikes it. He doesn't mention it to anyone, and other than *that*, other than the fact that Omar doesn't want to be in a car alone with him, it's almost normal. Omar still sits with them at lunch. They're still lab partners in chemistry. They just don't *talk*. It's like Mike makes Omar uncomfortable, and it's a really horrible feeling, to be on the receiving side of that.

And Meckles. Who the hell knows what's going on with Meckles? He isn't ignoring Mike, but he acts like he thinks Mike could jump him at any moment, and that *blows*.

Mike doesn't know what to do without Omar, though. It's dumb, but Omar's like the little voice in his head that tells him when he should think about showering or wearing a coat or when it's a bad idea to listen to Cam. Granted, that's nearly all the time, and it's not like Mike ever really takes his advice, but Omar's always been there to check him. So if Omar's going radio silent about this, why does it feel so much like condemnation? Mike isn't doing anything wrong—logically he knows that—but Omar's making him feel like shit.

And he knows that this is unfair, that it's not even Wallace's fault, that this is no one's actual fault, but if Wallace doesn't stop looking at him like that, like Mike's *awesome*, Mike might just punch him in the face, Leoni be damned.

It's crazy, because a few days ago Mike had been so

naively happy, but he still knew this could happen. He knew it, so why does it still seem like such a fucking surprise?

"So, Mike," Wallace says, leaning a hip against his lab table as they're packing up at the end of chemistry. "I was thinking we could—"

"Can we not talk about this now?" Mike wants to crawl under the lab desk. Omar is stiff beside him, radiating disapproval, and Mike wants the world to just stop for a few minutes.

"What's wrong?" Wallace asks him.

"Nothing," Mike says, clenching his hands into fists. He watches Omar zip up his schoolbag and then silently slip out of the classroom.

Wallace shoves his own hands into his pockets, like he's suddenly feeling awkward, and right now, Mike just doesn't have the energy for this. He sighs in exasperation.

"Are you sure you're okay?" Wallace says.

He sounds so genuinely concerned that Mike forces a smile onto his face, lets it grow a little more real when one corner of Wallace's mouth curves up to match it. "I'm okay, just. There's some stuff that's pissing me off."

Wallace nods. "Okay."

"Yeah, so—"

"Do you want to get pizza after school tomorrow?" Wallace asks.

Mike tightens his grip on his book bag and starts toward the door. "I have to work till eight."

Wallace shrugs. "After."

"Maybe," Mike says, hedging. Pizza means Carmine's and probably the field hockey team; those harpies are vicious. He turns around, hooking his bag over his shoulder as he pushes the door open wider. "We'll see."

"Hey." Wallace catches his arm, hand on his elbow. When Mike half turns to look back at him, Wallace smiles, but his smile looks shaky, like he's unsure. "We're still on for Christmas Eve, right?"

Mike bobs his head. "Yeah, sure. I mean—probably."

Wallace forces his lips up further and firmer at the corners, but his eyes don't follow.

Mike regrets even saying probably. He *wants* to go. It's Evan Dando and it's *Wallace*. He *does* want to go, he just feels . . . he feels like all his limbs are hollow and his heart is pounding and it's motherfucking *stupid*, but he's suddenly terrified that this all means something that he's not ready for it to mean. "My grandmother might freak out about it, though," he says, lying. Nana would purse her lips and lecture him about using protection. "We're, um, supposed to spend the holidays with her and Gramps, over in Bridgeport." Bridgeport is two hours in the opposite direction of Philly, but it's still a shitty excuse.

"Well," Wallace says.

Mike still can't read his eyes. Or maybe he doesn't want to. He drops his gaze and watches Wallace's chest expand on an inhale.

"Maybe we should cancel, then," Wallace says.

Mike sort of hates himself for saying, "Yeah, maybe we should."

Mike walks his bike next to Serge and Jason on the way home from school.

Jason has his hands in his pockets and has been shooting Mike worried looks. It's not like Mike doesn't know *why*; he just doesn't want to deal with it.

But of course Serge asks, "So why aren't we just getting a ride with Omar?"

Mike tightens his hands around the bike's handlebars. "No reason."

Serge snorts. "Right."

Jason pointedly doesn't say anything. It simultaneously makes Mike want to hug him and punch him in the face.

By the time they reach his house, Mike has decided that he wants to get drunk. Mike wants to get so drunk he can't remember his name, or Wallace's name, or *Omar's* name. He wants to drink himself into a stupor and not come up for at least three days. That would be ace.

He snags his mom's bottle of cherry rum on their way through the kitchen and up to his room.

Jason says, "Are you sure—"

"Yes," Mike cuts him off. "Yes, I'm fucking sure I want

to get wasted, Jay. You're welcome to leave if you don't feel like watching me throw up all over myself."

Serge makes a face, but says, "Cool. Count me in."

"You're too young to drink," Mike says.

"Bullshit," Serge says.

Mike eyes him narrowly. "Your brother will kill me."

Serge smirks. "I sincerely doubt that," he says, which is wrong. So wrong, because Wallace will either beat him dead with a baseball bat or guilt him to death with those puppy-dog eyes, the ones that tell Mike that he might've broken his fucking heart.

Jason says, "I'm leaving," but he follows them up the stairs anyway.

"No, you're not," Mike says. Jason isn't leaving, because Jason has appointed himself honorary Omar, and likes to follow Mike around and tell him about all the stuff he shouldn't be doing. It sucks, but only because he isn't actually Omar.

Mike is such a sad, sorry fucker. He plops down on his bed and twists the cap off the bottle of rum. It burns all the way down to his stomach, and makes him almost instantly light-headed. He probably should have actually eaten lunch.

"This is a stupid idea," Jason says, taking the bottle as Mike passes it to him.

"Don't let Junior have any," Mike says, and Serge says, "Hey!" but, seriously, if Serge gets drunk on his watch *bad things will happen*. Mike knows this.

Jason takes a swig, grimacing, and then gives the rum back to Mike.

Mike lifts it in salute and says, "Cheers."

"A bake sale," Lisa says, sitting down next to him in math.

"What?" Mike says. He doesn't know how he's conscious. It feels like tiny, rampaging elephants are goring the inside of his skull with their tusks. He'd woken up that morning alone, on the floor of his bathroom—he vaguely remembers Jason telling him he was walking Serge home at some point. He hopes that doesn't mean Serge was too drunk to walk himself, but Mike's luck is not that good. He'd *barely* avoided a lecture from his mom, and his mom usually doesn't bother lecturing him about anything.

"We're having a bake sale," Lisa repeats. "To raise money for a vending machine in the cafeteria." She purses her lips. "Why do you look like something my cat hacked up?"

"Rum," Mike says. "Lots and lots of rum."

"I see," she says, slow and careful.

"No. No, you don't," Mike says. Lisa has been so busy with school and student council and Larson that Lisa hasn't seen *anything at all*.

She taps her fingers on the cover of her textbook. "Okay. Want to tell me what I don't see, then?"

Mike shakes his head, then immediately regrets it. He

swallows back bile that burns his throat like acid, and cra-
dles his pounding head in between his hands. "Fuck."

"Michael," Lisa says sharply, then mouths *later* when
Mr. Dougherty starts class.

Mike tries to make a break for it at the bell, but his hangover makes him slow, and Lisa grabs his arm and prods
him all the way down the foreign language hall to the auditorium.

"We're skipping class?" he asks. On the one hand, it
means he doesn't have to face Wallace just yet. On the other,
he'll be stuck with Lisa and Lisa's interrogation face for at
least an hour. Crap.

"You're telling me what's going on," she says. They slip
silently into the back of the dark auditorium and settle down
on the floor by the sound booth. She crosses her legs and
pulls her backpack onto her lap. "Now."

Mike falls back and sprawls out on the floor. There are
probably all kinds of gross things happening on the thin rug,
but he doesn't care. He wants to catch some awful disease
and die. Maybe then all his cells will stop throbbing. "I told
everybody."

There's a pause. "You told everybody what?" Lisa asks.

Mike throws an arm over his face. "The guys. I told Omar
and Meckles I was dating Wallace."

"Wait," she says. "Wait, hold up, you're dating *Rook*?
When did this happen?"

"Let's concentrate on the part where—where Omar *hates*

me, okay? How about we do that." Mike is not going to cry. Mike is super badass awesome and Mike is *totally* not going to cry.

Lisa makes a *pshaw* sound. "Omar doesn't hate you. That's impossible. You're seriously dating Rook?"

"*Was*, I don't know." He doesn't want to worry about that now. Right now he wants to wallow in misery, because his life *sucks*.

Lisa punches him in the thigh. "Tell me," she says.

"My life is over."

"That's crazy," Lisa says. "Stop being so pathetic. Now tell me about you dating Rook."

Mike sighs. "We had sex in his car and then went for ice cream." It's still awesome in retrospect, but he can't shake the feeling that if it hadn't happened, maybe Omar would still be talking to him. Christ, he hates himself.

"You had—oh Jesus," Lisa says. He can hear a hint of horrified amusement in her tone.

"Shut up."

"I don't see why you're so upset," Lisa says.

Mike drops his arm and props himself up on his elbows so he can look at her. She seems genuinely bewildered. "Did you miss the part about Omar?"

"No, but I don't believe it," she says firmly.

"You don't," Mike says.

"No," she says. "I don't." She shrugs a little. "I bet it's all a misunderstanding. Or religious angst. You know his dad's

uber Catholic, right? Like a yay-Jesus wilderness survival-
ist. You know Omar was raised *weird*, they've got dead animals all over their basement. Omar thinks you're pretty
awesome, though. He always has."

"Well, he—wait, um. He does?" That's news to Mike, actually. *Omar's* the awesome one; Mike's always felt sort of
privileged to hang out with such a cool dude. Huh.

"Yeah," Lisa says, grinning at him. "I don't get it either."

Dotty and Lenny flank him at the library table he's claimed
in study hall, and Mo takes the seat across from him, leaning back in her chair with one eyebrow raised.

Dotty says, "This is getting ridiculous. Even Mo thinks
so."

Mo nods, and Lenny says, "Super ridiculous."

"What is?" Mike says, even though he's pretty sure he
knows the answer. Chemistry class had been weird. Mike had
pretty much spent the entire period trying to ignore Omar
ignoring him and avoiding Wallace's glare.

"You and Rook," Dotty says.

The three of them stare at him while Mike tries not to
squirm.

Finally, Mo covers her mouth with a hand and says, voice
muffled, "Oh my god."

Mike ducks his head. He can feel his face burning, even
though she can't possibly mean what he thinks she means

by that. It's not that obvious, or more people would have picked up on it by now. Right?

Except she says, "Oh my god," again, and, "You're blushing," which is unfair, since he hadn't been blushing until she'd said the first *oh my god*, but whatever.

"I don't get it," Lenny says.

Dotty narrows her eyes. "Wait."

Mo leans forward, hands gripping the edge of the table, and hisses, "You and *Rook*."

"No *way*, seriously?" Lenny squeals. She sounds *delighted*. She sounds like all her dreams have come true, because she's clearly demented.

Mike buries his head in his arms. "I don't want to talk about it."

"Too bad, you *totally* have to talk about it," Lenny says.

"Or we could just ask Rook."

Mike jerks upright. "No."

Dotty grins evilly. He seriously hates cheerleaders.

"You can't say anything to Wallace. This is—" He wants to say *private*, but that isn't really the right word. He just doesn't want to make this situation worse than he's already making it, and letting Wallace think he's talking about him behind his back, however inadvertent, would suck. "—not a big deal," he ends up saying.

Mo slumps forward and rests her chin on an open palm. She says, "I can't believe you're *gay*." She isn't scandalized, but there's a hint of disbelief in her voice that gives

Mike a vaguely gratified feeling—until she stares at him for a beat too long, and then he kicks her in the shin under the table.

"I'm bi," he says, because he might as well. He's not hiding anything at this point. "And shut *up*."

Mo says, "Mike—"

"Shut up, shut up, just stop *talking*, okay?" Mike is going to go motherfucking postal if everyone doesn't just leave him alone, right now.

Dotty raises her hands, fingers spread. "Whoa, whoa, calm down," she says, eyes wide.

Mike takes a deep breath that leaves his body strangely achy, and he doubles over, banging his forehead on the wooden table. "Ow," he says softly. He's sick to his stomach, dehydrated, there's a rhythmic pounding behind his eyes, and he has two more hours of school to struggle through, and then *five more hours* of work at the House of Cheese.

Someone pats him lightly on the back.

He just knows they're all having a silent conversation about him with their eyebrows.

As long as they're quiet, though, he's going to let it slide.

Work goes about as well as it can when the smell of cheese brings back all of Mike's earlier queasiness. Luckily, Uncle Louie lets him nap on the couch in the storeroom for most of his shift—it pays to be family. He's doubly lucky that

Mark is working, not Leoni, because he's pretty sure he wouldn't live through the night.

At the end of the shift, Mike pulls on his jacket and steps out the front door of the shop, and there's Wallace, leaning on the metal stand next to Mike's bike. There's a pool of yellow from the streetlight, but Mike can still see Wallace's breath, spooling out like smoke.

"Hey," Wallace says.

Mike swallows down a groan. He doesn't feel like dealing with this shit right now, because Wallace is mad at him and Mike is absolutely sure he deserves it. "Yeah?"

Wallace shoves his hands in the pockets of his hoodie. "You got my brother drunk," he says gruffly. Mike should have been prepared for that, but he kind of wasn't, anyway. He'd mostly thought Wallace would be angry for the whole brush-off thing Mike's been giving him.

"Correction," Mike says after a moment. "He got himself drunk. I told him to go away and leave my rum alone."

Wallace's lips thin. "Okay."

"Yeah, so, is that all?" Mike's in a really shitty mood, his head hurts, and he just wants to go home and sleep for two days straight. Maybe he can convince his mom he's got the flu.

"No," Wallace says, and here it comes. Wallace is going to call Mike on his crap. But instead, Wallace just says, "I thought maybe we could get some pizza. Or ice cream." One corner of his mouth quirks up.

Mike says, "Are you kidding me?" because he's *stunned.*
Can't Wallace take a hint?

Wallace lets out a noisy breath. "Mike, I don't know what
I did, but—"

"You didn't do anything," Mike says. "I just can't—I can't
deal with this right now, okay?" He waves a hand around.
"I don't want to go out with you."

Wallace's jaw clenches. "You don't."

"I . . ." Mike stuffs his hands deep in his pockets, looks
up at the night sky. The corners of his eyes water, catching
on the edge of the halogen light. "Not right now," he says.
He thinks—he *knows* he wants—something. Something too
scary to name, something that he can't even think about,
not while he's trying to figure out how to fix this thing
between him and Omar. Between him and Meckles, even.
They've all been friends for too long for him to just fuck them
over for Rook motherfucking *Wallace.*

He wants to say all that to Wallace, to tell him *wait.* But
he doesn't, and Wallace barks out an unfunny laugh, and
when Mike looks over at him again, Wallace has a hand over
his eyes. Mike watches as he drags it down over his mouth
and chin. He sees that the line of Wallace's lips is hard and
the light in his eyes is damning, and Mike thinks that if he
doesn't fix this *right now,* if he doesn't open his mouth and
say something—anything—to make that expression go
away, then he's never going to get the chance again.

He stays there frozen for fuck knows how long after silently watching Wallace walk away.

Mike ends up on Cam's front stoop with his bike leaning against his shins and the nub of a cigarette burning his fingers. He drops it when he hears the door open behind him, and Cam says, "Zack told me you were lurking."

He sits down next to him on the step, pushing the bike out of the way.

Mike watches the back wheel spin lazily, rubbing at his bottom lip.

"What's up?" Cam says.

Mike shakes his head. "Nothing. Everything." *My life's a disaster,* he doesn't say, but he thinks Cam can read between the lines. Cam's observational skills are usually on par with a rabid squirrel, but he's known Mike for forever, and there are *some* perks to that.

"Look, teenagers are all assholes," Cam says. "Selfish, jerkface douche bags, Mike. You seriously think high school means *anything* in the grand scheme of things? High school *sucks*, but once we're out of here, we're *gone*. Fuck everyone else, *I* don't give a damn, and neither should you."

Mike curls his hands over his knees. "Meckles is—"

"Meckles is scared of girls, dude, why would gay guys be any different? Wait him out, he'll come around."

"What about Omar?" Mike says. His fingers are cold, and he rubs them harshly over the denim covering his thighs.

"Yeah." Cam makes a face. "Gotta admit, Omar shocked the shit out of me, too. I don't know what's going on there. Fuck, I'm not even sure *he* knows."

"Right." Mike nods. Thinking about Omar's silent freak-out still makes his chest tighten so hard he feels a little like he wants to throw up. If Omar's as lost as Cam thinks he is, though—maybe it's something they can work through.

Cam drops an arm around Mike's shoulders and pulls him in for an extended bro-hug. With his mouth close to Mike's temple, he says, "I wouldn't give a fuck if you only got hard-ons for unicorns, dude." Then he ruffles Mike's hair and shoves him away. "Now cheer up, gaybird, it's not all bad. You've got a hot boyfriend, right?"

Mike swallows hard. *Not really,* he wants to say, but the words get stuck in his throat.

He fucked that up royally, too.

eighteen.

Held the week before Christmas, Cam's annual birthmas party—*a celebration of the baby Jesus as well as the day Cam was born*, it says on the invitation—is generally smaller than and not nearly as epic as Cam's end-of-the-summer blowout or his Halloween bash. This is the first year Mike's ever *dreaded* it, though.

It's at Meckles' place, because Cam has a thing against hosting his own birthday party, and Mike is the only one out on the back patio. It's cold out, and Mike can hardly feel the fingers hanging on to his cigarette. He's not hiding, but he can see how Girl Meckles might think that when she finds him.

She flicks on the yard light before opening the sliding glass door. Music and laughter spill out from where almost everyone is crowded into the living room. Mike can picture everybody in their hideous Christmas sweaters—Cam never lets anyone inside without one—drinking fully spiked eggnog and hot chocolate, and eating Mom Meckles' gingersnap cookies. Later, they'll sing carols around Jason's keyboard. It's completely lame, but Mike usually loves it anyway.

Deanna has a pale blue parka on, a knit cap pulled down almost over her eyes. She fumbles a mitten off and grabs Mike's cigarette, taking a quick, shivery drag.

"You know that Shawn has a crush on you," she says, breathing out, wisps of smoke snaking up over her head.

It takes a slow second for Mike to realize she's talking about *Meckles*. He chokes out, *"What?"*

She shrugs. "Not, like, *romantic*," she says, and hell, she could have *led* with that and saved him the mini heart attack then. "A man-crush. A bromantic crush. It's cute. He's had it for years, but you being gay kind of made him freak out about it."

"That's so dumb," Mike says, but he doesn't really mean it. It's dumb, yeah, for Meckles to think his, uh, *man-crush* on a gay or bi dude makes *him* gay, too, but it's not dumb in the way that it could actually happen. Look at *Mike's* fucking life.

"He still stutters around Dotty," Deanna says, "and they've been officially dating for three weeks."

Mike wouldn't exactly call what Meckles and Dotty are doing dating. It's more like Dotty is stalking Meckles—showing up at the same places, hanging out with Deanna, leaving him notes in class, calling him constantly—and Meckles has decided to be more or less okay with that. The stuttering and blushing, well. Mike doubts Meckles will ever get over that.

Mike has been Meckles' friend since the second grade,

since the twins joined Boy Scouts. They let Deanna join unofficially, since they used to be codependent freaks who dressed alike and always held hands. Mike had legitimately thought they were aliens, at first. So even if Meckles has a *real* crush on him, which he *doesn't*, they've been over the awkward, shy, my-sister-talks-for-me crap since they bonded over derby cars and *Yu-Gi-Oh!*

"It's not the same thing," Mike says.

"No, it's not. He'll figure that out eventually," she says.

"Right," Mike says. He's kind of sick of exercising all this patience that he doesn't actually have.

Deanna squeezes his arm. "It sucks, Mike, but it'll be okay. Now, c'mon. I can't feel my nose, and Mom's gonna break out the pies soon. She made shoofly just for you."

It takes a big effort, but Mike tries to ignore the fact that Wallace is there, grin plastic and fake, that Leoni looks like he wants to kick the shit out of him, and that Meckles is laughing too loudly across the room. Omar has been avoiding looking him in the eyes, like maybe gay rays are going to leap out of them and wrestle him to the floor. He's equal parts hurt and angry—the anger has been building, because Mike honestly doesn't think he deserves this.

Eventually, Mike mostly shakes it off. They play party games, because it's tradition. Mo and Mike kick everyone's asses at charades, Jason pins a tail on Lenny's boobs, and

Mike sits Twister out, because he doesn't want to deal with touching limbs—or avoiding touching limbs—for the homophobes in the room. Instead, he sits with Dotty and Weedy Jim and Jules Fitzsimmons. Jules looks at him sourly—but she always looks like that, so it might not have anything to do with her judgment of the so-called evils of homosexuality. Whatever.

After the game falls apart—Cam humps Mo into a pile of giggles and declares himself the winner—Mike gets up to search for more pie and some Baileys for his hot chocolate. He hooks a candy cane into his mouth like a pipe and skirts the room, and he's so busy trying to be invisible that he doesn't notice the traffic jam around the kitchen doorway. He accidentally bumps Wallace with his elbow, and Wallace spins around. Now, Mike is faced with his reindeer sweater, red nose blinking on and off.

"Uh," Mike says. He shifts awkwardly on his feet, and he feels like he should maybe comment on the sweetness of Wallace's sweater, but he can't get his brain to work. They're way too close. Mike hasn't been this close to him since Wallace had his hand down his pants. That sort of makes a difference.

And then Lenny shouts, "Mistletoe!" at them, because she's an asshole.

Apparently they're standing under it, although Mike doubts it's *actual* mistletoe. It looks sort of like wilted lettuce. That isn't the problem, though. The problem is that

Wallace's face is so red he's steadily turning purple, and Mike is going to kill Lenny.

"Sorry," Mike says, voice low. He grits his teeth and moves around Wallace and into the kitchen, even though he isn't really hungry anymore.

Birthmas parties start early, with a delicious holiday dinner, and end late, with the sunrise. By dawn, every single surface area of Meckles' den is covered in bodies and pillows and blankets, and *National Lampoon's Christmas Vacation* is playing for the third time on the big-screen TV. There are maybe only four people still awake enough to watch it. As Mike leverages up from his spot by the couch and winds his way out of the room, he sees Cam's slit eyes gleam in the TV glow.

Mike slips outside the back door with an afghan and walks off the patio, down through Mom Meckles' dormant garden and out onto the frozen lawn. He settles down on the snow, back to the house, and watches the inky blue-black sky lighten to gray. The stars fade and the moon softens to a white stamp over the trees. On the other side of the house, he knows, the pink-and-orange streaks from the rising sun are probably just cresting slanted roofs. Back here, Mike's only getting the aftershocks.

In the end, the thing that Mike hates, that really gets him, is that it feels like everybody thinks they know who Mike should be.

Not just Omar and Meckles, but Lisa and J. J. and god-damn *Lenny*. And even Wallace. *Mike* doesn't know who he is, so why the hell does everyone else have to shove it down his throat?

He knows he's not really being fair. He feels bad for making it hard for everyone. He wishes he didn't have to. He knows that what's happened is more his own fault than anybody else's, but it doesn't really help, knowing that. He's letting it fester. He's letting Meckles' weird looks and Omar's silence and Wallace's hurt and anger get to him, and Cam's words of wisdom lose some of their appeal when Mike feels so fucking *alone*. And yet—

Mike isn't really alone. Not now, at least.

He hears a measured crunch of plodding footsteps through snow. A shadow falls across him and he feels someone sit down, settling into the cold beside him. He glances over and something jumps up high in his throat at the sight of Omar.

Omar just stares off across the long expanse of Meckles' backyard. He pushes his hoodie off his head and scratches his scalp, and Mike watches the thin, steady line of his mouth.

Finally, Omar says gruffly, "Sorry I'm being weird."

Mike's mouth is dry. His "It's okay" comes out raspy and hoarse. It's not actually okay, but he's fully aware that it *has* to be.

Omar snorts.

"What, you think *I'm* not being weird about this?" Mike says.

Omar turns and gives him a long look. "No. I know you are."

Mike bobs his head, then looks off into the distance again. The sky is blue-gray, lighter than it was five minutes ago, but still not light enough. Tufts of grass are starting to poke through the layer of snow—it's lasted too long already, anyhow, with cold air and overcast skies.

His jeans are soaked through and his ass is frozen and he doesn't feel like moving yet. Omar doesn't look like he wants to, either.

He feels like he has so much to say to Omar after over two weeks of silence, but he can't think of a single thing. "My mom was pretty cool about it. Everything," Mike says, for lack of anything else. He's grateful, fuck is he grateful, but he keeps waiting to stumble on her hiding somewhere, quietly sobbing about her big gay son, and how now she'll never have little Mikes to coddle. On the other hand, though, it's not like his mom had gone the conventional route with starting a family herself.

"Mike, nothing much fazes your mom," Omar says.

It's true. Mike's mom is unshakable. He thinks it's Cam's fault for desensitizing her to catastrophic events, like getting arrested, accidentally setting things on fire, and self-inflicting deep tissue wounds.

Omar shrugs with one shoulder and says, "She loves you."

"Yeah, well. I thought you loved me, too, asshole." His cheeks heat, because he's totally fishing here. He's not ashamed to admit that. There's still a big ball of hurt sitting like a stone in his stomach, and he really wants Omar to make it go away. He doesn't think that's asking for too much.

"I know." Omar sighs. He rubs his palms over his eyes, pressing them into the sockets, curling his fingers up over his temples, the dark, rough stubble from his hair growing back in. Mike watches his thumb sweep over the dip of smooth skin in front of his ear, back and forth, methodical. "I'm trying really hard to understand this."

Mike nods, even though Omar isn't looking. Mike's trying really hard to understand this, too. He says, "It's not—you get this doesn't affect *you*, right?"

Omar doesn't say anything.

Mike pushes a little. He says, "You're not going to catch gay *cooties* or something. This is about me, and how much I—"

"If you say 'like cock,' I'm going to punch you in the head," Omar says. There's a tightness around his eyes when he looks at him, but the words still make Mike grin a very small grin—they're so *normal*.

"Okay," Mike says. Okay. Things aren't perfect, they're not the same, but maybe they're just a little better.

nineteen.

"You have to fix things with Rook," Lisa says after they're sitting in a booth at Carmine's with a couple slices of pizza each.

Mike says, "Why?" even though he *knows* why. He maybe doesn't have the same reasons as Lisa, who thinks they're adorable together and that a sad Wallace is just awful, but he misses Wallace a lot more than he thought he ever would.

Wallace has always been *something* to him. Enemy or friend or more. There's a Wallace-shaped hole in his life, and in some ways it's worse than the estrangement with Omar, because at least Omar was still *there*. Quiet and subdued, but there. Mike feels a little guilty thinking like that—that maybe it means Wallace is more to him than Omar—except that's a fucking joke, because they're both important to Mike in different ways. Maybe, now that Omar is starting to make an effort with him, that just makes the hole Wallace has left seem even more pronounced.

Christ, Mike is *totally fucking whipped*. By everyone.

Lisa gives him a *duh* look and ignores him. She says, "This is what you do: you apologize."

Mike thinks it can't be that easy. Plus, Mike obviously has some major issues. Why would Wallace want to deal with all of that? "Apologize," he echoes dully.

"Say you're sorry. Simple and effective."

Mike looks down at his pizza. He's not really all that hungry anymore. He wasn't all that hungry to begin with, actually, but Lisa had shown up at his house and tricked him into taking her out to dinner. "This isn't like I was a dick to him only *once*," Mike says. He recognizes that he's pretty much always treated Wallace like garbage. Not that he hasn't had his reasons, but still.

"And yet," Lisa says, "he still asked you out." She nudges him with her feet under the table. "Do it."

"*Lisa.*"

"Do it. Do it, do it, dooooo it," Lisa says, grinning, because she knows she's won, the harpy.

"Do what?" Cam says, sliding onto the bench next to Mike. He takes Mike's uneaten slice, rolls it up and takes a huge bite. It's like Cam has some sixth sense for when people are having private conversations and pizza.

"Tell Rook he's sorry for breaking his heart," Lisa says.

"I didn't break his heart," Mike says.

"I don't know, dude, he seems pretty fucking tragic," Cam says. "You should tell your hot boyfriend you're sorry."

Mike splutters like a cartoon character, because this is his life. "He's not my—would you stop calling him *hot*?"

"Jealous?" Cam grins.

Mike palms his face and groans. "I fucking hate you guys."

Cam pats his back. "Don't worry, Mike, he's totally not my type."

Rosie stares at him across the kitchen table. It's a Sunday, so she has a hot dog and mashed potatoes and a pile of peas that she may or may not eat, depending on Sandwich's mood.

Mike has a Pop-Tart.

Their mom is at a meeting, the last one, she swears, before the new year. She'll be all theirs for the holidays. Mom's always great with Christmas, though. She and Rosie decorated the whole house while he was at Cam's birthmas party, they have a huge tree in the den, and they got out the matching Tate elf hats that Mom makes them wear every Christmas morning. Rosie has hers on already, red-and-green striped with bells on the tip.

Mike's not feeling very festive, though.

Rosie tips her head to one side, then the other, jangling the bells.

Finally, Mike says, "What?"

Rosie frowns. She says, "Who's your boyfriend?"

Mike seriously hates his nana. "No one," he says.

"Sure?" she asks.

Mike shrugs and stares down at his half-eaten brown sugar cinnamon Pop-Tart. He wants to tell her that it's complicated, but she's six, and complications are pretty much lost on her.

"Sandwich says you're sad," she says. She shifts up onto her knees and leans her elbows on the table, narrowly missing her mashies. "Are you sad 'cause you don't have a boyfriend?"

"Uh." Yes and no. Her earnest face kind of makes him want to laugh.

"You should find one then," she says decisively. "Nana's always right."

"She told you to say that," Mike says, and he can't believe his grandmother is meddling in his love life by way of his little sister. That's just *wrong*. Christ, she probably put her up to this entire conversation.

Rosie just pushes her plate away and says, "Okay, I'm done."

"You barely ate a fourth of your hot dog," Mike says, but he drops what's left of his Pop-Tart onto her plate and gets to his feet.

"I saved room for ice cream," she says.

"Good thinking," he says, and then she shouts, "Ice cream and *Rudolph*!" and Mike finds himself spending the rest of the night sprawled on the couch with Rosie tucked into his side, marathoning claymation Christmas movies.

She falls asleep before Mom gets home. Usually, Mike will poke her awake and follow her zombie walk up the stairs, making sure she brushes her teeth before falling into bed. This time, he just hefts her up—she's getting heavy—and tucks her under her bedcovers and turns on the night-slash-hermit-crab-cage light and softly ruffles her hair.

She reaches up sleepily and wraps small fingers over his wrist. "You should be happy," she says, and fuck, she's right—Mike *should* be. He's got an awesome little sister, a cool mom, good friends, mostly, even the ones currently being weird, and he's got a guy who likes him, who deserves an apology. His life is pretty fucking *charmed*, actually. Maybe he's just being a cranky asshole brat.

"Thanks, Rosalinda," he says softly. "Sleep tight."

Mike thinks it would be a bad idea to approach Wallace at school—public humiliation is the last thing he needs—so he reluctantly trudges down the street to Wallace's house Monday afternoon.

Serge opens the door when he knocks.

Serge is scowling at him, which isn't all that unusual, except for once his eyes look just as unfriendly as his mouth. Great. Another friend who hates him. He should have counted on that happening.

"Hey," Mike says, rocking back on his heels. "Is your brother home?"

Serge slams the door in his face.

Mike grimaces, bows his head and scuffs his sneakers on their welcome mat. He's contemplating knocking again when the door creaks and two booted feet step out onto the front stoop. Mike's gaze travels up Wallace's legs, takes in the wide, defensive stance. Wallace's face would be expressionless, except there's a twitch at the corner of his mouth. Not a happy twitch. A downward-curving twitch that makes Mike want to look away.

He doesn't, though. He stands his ground and says, "Wallace. Rook. I just wanted—"

"Now you call me Rook?" Wallace says, incredulous.

Mike feels like he's been sucker punched by Leoni again, but he's not sure why. "Sorry. I don't have to. I mean, I won't." He glances over Wallace's shoulder and back again. "I'm fucking this up."

"You've already fucked this up, Tate," Wallace says, voice hard.

Mike bobs his head. "I know. Fuck, I know. It's just—I'm sorry."

"You already said that."

"Not for your *name*, Wallace," Mike says. "I'm sorry about everything. This is just really hard for me. This guy thing." It's new and scary, he wants to say. He wants to shake Wallace until he gets that. Until he sees how fucking difficult it is.

"What, you think I'm just *okay* with this?" Wallace says, eyes wide with disbelief.

"Yes," Mike says, waving a hand around. He's not screeching or anything, and Wallace has no business wincing like that.

Wallace shoves a hand through his hair. "Fuck," he says. "Fuck, Mike. I'm—I'm *terrified*. And you just—everybody—you act like you're just shrugging on a new coat."

"What?"

"Like, like it's maybe tight on you, but if you wiggle a little it'll stretch to fit."

"What?" Mike's lost, are they having the same conversation?

"You! You're *owning* this," Wallace nearly shouts. "I haven't even told my dad yet."

Mike stares at Wallace. "What?" he says, one more time, for posterity, and then he starts laughing. Huge, almost forceful laughs, from deep down in his belly, the kind that make his stomach and throat hurt, the kind that make his eyes tear and his nose run. He vaguely takes in the way Wallace shifts on his feet, scowling, arms crossed over his chest.

"It's not funny," Wallace snaps, which just means it's *hysterical*.

And sad. So, so sad.

Finally, Mike catches his breath and Wallace's arms, fingers hooking into his elbows. He says, "You kissed me. Twice. In public. We had sex in your car. In a packed *parking lot*, Wallace, are you kidding me?"

Wallace's arms slip down to hang at his sides, shifting Mike's grip to his forearms. "That wasn't—"

"That was you owning the fuck out of this," Mike says, shaking him a little. He doesn't know exactly why he finds it so funny, because it *is* serious. Serious fucking business; this out and proud shit takes balls Mike still doesn't think he's grown yet. Cam would just tell him to nut up, but Cam can kiss his tight, homosexual ass. Cam doesn't have to worry about anything except whether Girl Meckles will forgive him for whatever stunt he's trying to pull that week.

"My friends know," Mike says. "My mom found my porn, and my nana decided to make a Thanksgiving celebration out of it. One of my best friends isn't really talking to me right now, and another one probably thinks I'm going to Hell. I'm not in control of this, Wallace. You don't get to have a monopoly on being *scared* here."

But neither, Mike realizes, does *he*. It's kind of really freeing, that thought.

Wallace nods a little. Mike watches the slow slide of his Adam's apple as he swallows, the way tension sort of seeps out of the line of his shoulders, even though the skin around his eyes still looks thin and tight. "So what do we do, then?"

Mike shrugs, drops his hands. "Beats the fuck out of me. I don't think we *have* to do anything."

"Right," Wallace says. He looks at Mike, and whatever he sees there—Mike isn't sure what he's projecting, but when Wallace reaches out to rub a hand over Mike's jaw, up over the still sore spot where Leoni had nearly cracked his face in two, Mike finds himself smiling at the warm press of his fingers.

"You owe me a date, though," Mike says. He's not sure that's true. It's actually more like Mike owes *Wallace* a date, but it doesn't matter.

Wallace grins a very small grin back.

twenty.

The last week before Christmas break is weird. It's weird primarily because of Meckles and Wallace. Not even Wallace, actually. Wallace, with his awkwardness and oddly shy smiles, is a very small, minuscule part of the weirdness that is the week before Christmas. Meckles makes sure of this.

Omar has been picking him up for school again, which is great, since he'd probably freeze his balls off trying to bike it. Conversation is a little stilted, but Mike appreciates the effort.

On Wednesday, Meckles gets bookended by Cam and Jason at the lunch table. Cam's eating everyone's pudding, and Jay is studiously cutting his peanut butter and jelly sandwich with a knife and fork. They're both abnormally close to Meckles, like they're pinning him in, and Meckles is staring at Mike directly across the suspiciously sticky length of faux wood.

Staring at him with *purpose*. It's Meckles' I'm-listening-to-Temple-of-the-Dog look, half awe and half like he wants to tongue-kiss Eddie Vedder. Which is *so appropriate*; Meckles really does have a stupid crush on him. Meckles' cheeks are flushed and his fingers are white-knuckled around his Coke can.

"You have got to be kidding me," Mike says. It's not that he didn't believe Deanna, it's just that he didn't actually fucking *believe* her.

"It's not a big deal," Meckles says quickly. "It's not—I'm not calling it a *man-crush*, okay."

Mike grins at him and says, "I am never ever letting you live this down, you realize that, right?"

Meckles mutters, "Shut the fuck up, asshole," and shoves half his sandwich in his mouth.

Cam snickers.

"What's going on?" Omar says, sitting down next to Mike.

"Nothing," Meckles says, digging an elbow into Cam's side.

An elbow jab never stopped Cam from doing anything ever, though. Mike kicks him really hard in the shin.

Cam yelps and jerks back in his chair. The chair fails to jerk back with him, though, and it tips over backward. His feet catch the edge of the table as he topples, spilling Jason's juice box and Meckles' can of soda, and Omar surveys them all with a deep frown.

"Nothing," Omar says, skeptical.

"Yep, nothing at all," Mike says, nodding at him, doing his best to radiate peace and calm and innocence, because there is no way he's going to bring up to Omar the fact that

Meckles has a giant man-crush on Mike. He doubts it works—Omar has always been able to see what Mike's face is trying hard not to say—but Omar just smiles at him, shaking his head. At some point, probably when Omar accidentally catches Mike sucking face with some dude, everyone is going to freak out all over again, but Mike's content, for right then, to just let it lie.

Mike is not scared of Serge. It's really stupid to be scared of *Serge*, right, but there's just something about him that's currently creeping Mike out.

"Dude, there's something wrong with Wallace's brother," Cam says, hunching his shoulders as a gust of wind whips around the abandoned Sears.

Mike says, "He's trying to intimidate me." *That fucker.* It's totally not working, either. Serge can glare at him as much as he wants; he still just looks like an angry fluff-ball kitten in oversized pants and a beanie. A really, *really* angry fluff-ball kitten. Mike has to fight the urge to cover his junk—he happens to know that Serge is lethal with his Doc Martens.

"It's totally working," Cam says.

"Fuck you," Mike says, but there isn't any heat to his words.

It's freezing at the Lot, and Mike's not sure what they're doing there, anyway. Deanna's sprawled on a mound of plowed snow, Omar is sitting on the roof of his van, knees pulled up to his chin, Serge is standing with Meckles and Jay only a little ways away from Mike and Cam.

Otherwise, the Lot's practically empty. There's only the faint sound of skateboarders from down by the Payless.

Cam knocks their shoulders together. "I bet it's because you've been dicking around with his brother." Cam snickers, and Mike kind of wants to punch his face in.

Instead, he just shoves his fists into his armpits and shivers. It's *cold*.

"He's probably going to give you the 'break my brother's heart and I'll rip out your lungs' speech," Cam says, grinning wider. "I will fucking *pay* to see that. I'll give you my firstborn if you let me video it and put it up on YouTube. That kid's like a miniature pony with an attitude; you just want to pet him and put bows in his mane while he tries to snap your fingers like carrots."

Mike huffs a laugh. "What the fuck, Cam?"

The thing is, though, that Mike hasn't talked to Serge since Serge slammed the door in his face. Mike and Wallace might have made up, but Serge is, like, a sensitive soul, and as unforgiving as a mule. Mike has seen his Revenge List of people who've wronged him; it goes all the way back to kindergarten.

"Christ," Mike mutters under his breath. He does not want to do this.

He's got an obligation, though. Serge is his friend, he's *all* their friend. He's been officially brought into the fold, he can tell by the affectionate look in Deanna's eyes. Serge is also Wallace's little brother, so he can either get over whatever the fuck is bothering him or punch Mike in the gut and move on. Mike should probably give him the opportunity to do both.

Cam pushes him in the back with his elbow, making Mike stumble, and Mike says, "Fuck this," and stalks over to where Meckles seems to be teaching Jason how to beatbox.

Serge cocks his head at him, expression petulant.

Mike rolls his eyes. He jerks his head to the side and says, "Come on."

"What?" Serge sneers, but follows him over toward the sidewalk.

"You have some sort of problem with me now?" Mike says when they're out of earshot of everyone else. He crosses his arms over his chest.

"No," Serge says, scowling.

"Bullshit." Mike narrows his eyes, staring at him, until Serge breaks and huffs a breath and sort of throws his arms up in the air like a hilarious Muppet.

"I'm just, like—" Serge glares at Mike, then down at his shoes. "Are we still gonna hang out?"

Mike blinks. Not at all what he was expecting. "What?"

"You, um—you used me for my brother, so—"

"Wait, *what*? Why would I—?" Mike pinches the bridge of his nose. He kind of wants to laugh, but it's probably a bad time. "Dude, we're *friends*. That has nothing to do with your brother."

Serge gives him a skeptical look.

"No, for real, pissing Wallace off for a while there was fun, but that's not why"—he can't believe he has to do this—"I *like* you." This is so humiliating. "You're, uh, cool, you know, I like hanging out with you, the guys like hanging out with you." Mike shrugs. He likes watching cartoons with him and Teeny and Rosie; he likes arguing with him about ice cream flavors and Bruce Willis movies—but not music, because Serge stubbornly refuses to admit he's wrong about everything, which makes Mike's head hurt. "I don't see what the problem is."

Serge nods his head slowly, like he's still not entirely sure. "Okay."

"Okay?"

"Yeah," Serge says, stuffing his hands in his pockets. "Fine."

Mike slaps his shoulder. "Good. Now stop being a pussy and go dare Cam to stick an icicle up his nose." Cam will do it, too. There'll probably be a walrus impression involved, it'll be great.

Serge makes a face.

"No, seriously, just make sure he doesn't accidentally stab his brain."

• • •

Mike is feeling pretty good about Friday. In fact, he's feeling so fantastic about Friday, he shows up with a smile on his face and everything, because it's the last school day before break, and only two days before Christmas.

This good mood, predictably, only lasts until just before homeroom. Wallace corners him at his locker with a sheepish look and an envelope.

"What's this?" Mike asks when Wallace shoves the envelope into his hands.

Wallace scratches his forearm and shrugs. "It's, uh—"

Mike flips open the flap and peeks inside. It's the tickets to see Evan Dando. He looks up at Wallace again, a bad feeling in the pit of his stomach. "What?"

"You should take Cam," Wallace says.

"I should," Mike says dumbly. Right. Of course.

Wallace smiles at him, though. "You'd probably have more fun with Cam," he says reasonably.

"Right," Mike says. He'd crush the envelope in his palm except it's *Evan Dando* tickets, he'll probably want to frame the stubs once he's done having his heart ground underneath the sole of Wallace's size-eleven shoes. And then he mentally shakes himself and stops being so *stupid*, because Wallace is right—he probably *would* have more fun with Cam.

Cam knows all the words to the songs, and he won't care if maybe Mike tears up a little bit during "The Great Big No," and he'd definitely hang with him outside the venue afterward for as long as it takes Evan Dando to appear.

But that doesn't mean—well, Mike isn't exactly sure what it *means*, but he still wants to go with Wallace, anyway. Shit.

Mike nods. He says, "I'm pretty sure I should take you, though," and watches Wallace's smile get *bigger*. Mike doesn't even know, but it's kind of infectious.

"You're sure?" Wallace says. He ducks his head, and the tops of his cheeks are pink, because he's obviously a giant girl.

"Yeah, Wallace," Mike says, hooking his thumbs into his jean pockets, pleased, because obviously *he's* a giant fucking girl too, "I'm sure."

twenty-one.

Christmas Eve is cold and quiet. By the time the concert lets out, the street is nearly deserted, and the people pouring out of the Theater of the Living Arts are surprisingly hushed. It hasn't snowed in Philly yet, but the air is frigid. Most of the shops have closed for the holiday, so it seems like it's just them awake in the usually busy neighborhood.

It's not dark, even though it's after midnight, because Christmas lights are strung up everywhere, and the skies are inky pink above them.

Mike feels good. He feels even better when Wallace hooks his arm through his and tugs him down the sidewalk, steering them toward the car and the river. The crowd follows, mellow and subdued. Or maybe they're following the crowd. Either way, it's nice.

Calling his grandmother had been completely embarrassing, but ultimately worth it, he thinks. She'd been smug— he could hear it through the phone—and then she'd said, "Let's talk about condoms," and Mike had totally been expecting that, of course, even though he'd already had the safe sex talk with his mom, thanks, and didn't need one from his nana, too. When he'd told her that, she'd said, "I'm sure," and, "I hope she reminded you to use one during fellatio as well, Michael," and Mike had seriously considered giving up all possibility of blow jobs ever, Jesus Christ, but then he realized that's crazy talk.

Anyway, this night has been worth all that, he's pretty sure.

Wallace says, "Enjoy it?"

"Fuck, yeah!" Evan Dando is a rock god. Everyone who doesn't think so can go fuck themselves. The concert had been freaking *magical*; Mike's sure he'd had stars in his eyes through the entire set, and Wallace only teased him a little for shouting all the words to "Confetti" along with the rest of the audience.

Wallace laughs, then tugs Mike closer and wraps his arm around his back. Their hips bump together when they walk, and Mike doesn't mind. This having a hot boyfriend thing is pretty fucking sweet, actually; Cam was right.

He is never telling Cam that ever. It's bad enough that he's successfully brought the fanny pack back.

Someone pushes past them, knocking into Mike's shoulder, and Wallace tenses all along his side, because this whole out and proud in public thing is still weird, Mike can admit that.

The guy just arches an eyebrow at them, says, "Sorry, man," and tugs his girlfriend along by way of their clasped hands. It's the wonder of Evan Dando and his acoustic guitar, Mike thinks. All is right with the world.

Wallace relaxes against him. He drops his arm but twines their fingers together, and Mike totally doesn't care that they're now holding hands in public—something he swore he'd never do, with *anyone*—because Mike's fingers are cold, and fuck everyone, anyway.

He hums "It's a Shame About Ray," idly watching his breath smoke and disappear, and Wallace suddenly tightens his grip, twisting his other hand in Mike's coat to swing him into a quick kiss, his lips softly grinning.

Mike blinks up at him.

"What was that for?" he asks, because people are still spilling around them, murmuring, talking, laughing. Mike can feel eyes on them, curious.

Wallace shrugs, still grinning. "No reason."

There are no visible stars. There's smog and glittering lights from Camden's waterfront and the briny scent of the river, and Wallace is acting like they're the only people in the world. It's not true, not even for their current tiny corner of it, paused across the street from the parking lot, but for the moment, Mike doesn't really care. He doesn't think Wallace does, either.

"Okay, then," Mike says. He tugs on a curl of Wallace's hair that's fallen over his forehead. "Cool."

acknowledgments.

I want to give special thanks to my hus-band, Jesse, who serves as a deep well of cautionary high school tales, and has always given me endless and enthusiastic support in whatever I've chosen to do. And to Kerry Shallis, who would be the Cam to my Mike, if either of us were ever anything like Cam and Mike.

I'm also forever grateful to the amazingly talented Melissa Barr for putting up with all my writing panics and anxieties, for doling out the best advice, for being limitless in her encouragement, and for being my sounding board and brain-storming partner—you're such a good writer, and you've always helped me try to be one, too.

And, finally, enormous thanks to my wonderful editor Connie Hsu, and everyone else at Roaring Brook Press who loved this story enough to help me spit-shine and polish it and present it to the world.